THE TABLES
OF THE LAW

Thomas Mann

THE TABLES
OF THE LAW

*Translated by Marion Faber
and Stephen Lehmann*

Afterword by Michael Wood

PAUL DRY BOOKS
Philadelphia   2010

First Paul Dry Books edition, 2010

Paul Dry Books, Inc.
Philadelphia, Pennsylvania
www.pauldrybooks.com

Originally published as *Das Gesetz*
Copyright © 1960, 1974 S. Fischer Verlag GmbH,
Frankfurt am Main

Translation, Introduction, and
Afterword copyright © 2010 Paul Dry Books, Inc.

Printed in the United States of America

Library of Congress Cataloging-in-Publication Data

Mann, Thomas, 1875–1955
　[Gesetz. English]
　The tables of the law / Thomas Mann ; translated by Marion Faber
and Stephen Lehmann. — 1st Paul Dry Books ed.
　　p. cm.
　Originally published as: Das gesetz, 1944.
　ISBN 978-1-58988-057-3 (alk. paper)
　1. Moses (Biblical leader)—Fiction. I. Faber, Marion. II. Lehmann,
Stephen. III. Title.
　PT2625.A44G5 2010
　833'.912—dc22

　　　　　　　　　　　　　　　　　　　　　　　2010003618

Contents

Introduction

In 1943, when Thomas Mann wrote *The Tables of the Law* (*Das Gesetz*), he was already a world-renowned literary figure, author of the family saga *Buddenbrooks,* for which he had been awarded the 1929 Nobel Prize in Literature, and *The Magic Mountain.* He was sixty-seven years old and living in California, ten years into his self-exile from Germany. His diaries note that he started writing on January 18, two days after an entry about the fighting in Stalingrad, following a few weeks of preparatory reading that included the Bible itself, of course, and also Elias Auerbach's two-volume *Desert and Promised Land* (*Wüste und Gelobtes Land*) and Voltaire's *Candide.* The story, which Mann called his "Moses fantasy" and his "$1000 *Novelle*"—the only piece of fiction he ever wrote on commission—was finished just eight weeks later, on March 13. He described it as "a quick improvisation," "a diversion" that he wrote "quickly and easily, as it were for pleasure," immediately after completing his mammoth *Joseph* tetralogy. "It was my artistic intention," he said in a letter (in English), "in the Joseph books as well as in the

Moses story, to bring these far and legendary figures close to the modern reader in an intimate, natural and convincing manner. This required much phantasy and a certain affectionate brand of humor . . ."

The Tables of the Law grew out of a proposal by the Austrian-born publisher, impresario, librettist, and literary agent Armin L. Robinson to produce a movie that would dramatize to the world the Nazi desecration of the Mosaic Decalogue, which represented the very foundation of civilization and morality. Robinson discussed the idea with Mann and even brought him along to a meeting with Hollywood mogul Louis B. Mayer, the head of MGM. The movie didn't materialize, but Robinson went forward with a proposal to gather the contributions of ten writers—one per commandment—into a book. Mann agreed to write an introductory essay and signed a contract for one thousand dollars.

Mann's introduction quickly evolved into a long story that he sent to Robinson with the offer (how sincere we can't know) to cut it radically. Robinson, not surprisingly, was happy to accept it as Mann had given it to him and decided to use it as the first of the ten stories in the anthology. After a few false starts, *Das Gesetz* found a translator in George Marek—at the time a music writer, later an RCA executive—who worked under Mann's supervision.

The Ten Commandments: Ten Short Novels of Hitler's War Against the Moral Code was published by Simon and

Schuster in time for Christmas 1943. Herman Rauschning, who had been an early Nazi but by 1943 was a convinced opponent and a fellow refugee, wrote the preface. He set the stage for the collection's stories by describing a meeting he had attended with Hitler, Goebbels, Julius Streicher, and others: "The day will come," Hitler is supposed to have said, "when I shall hold up against these commandments the tables of a new law . . . Against the so-called ten commandments, against them we are fighting." (Historians now believe that Rauschning's account has little basis in fact.)

Mann's story was the first in the collection. An international roster of authors, some of them at the time almost as prominent as Mann himself, wrote the other nine: Rebecca West, Franz Werfel, John Erskine, Bruno Frank, Jules Romains, André Maurois, Sigrid Undset, Hendrik Willem Van Loon, and Louis Bromfield. Mann claimed to be impressed by the lineup but in the end was contemptuous of the others' contributions. The one-thousand-dollar fee, he commented, seemed to have been their only inspiration, and none of the efforts was worth it; he regarded the collection as a "failure" from which his own story stood out.

The writing of *The Tables of the Law* turned out to be the easy part. In the months and years that followed, Mann's diaries and correspondence track the seemingly endless bickering among publishers, agents, and translators over who owned what rights to the text. "The stupidest and most muddled business that has ever happened to any work of mine" is how he characterized the situation to his German-language publisher Gottfried Bermann Fischer.

The disputes arose when Bermann Fischer, Alfred Knopf (Mann's U.S. publisher), Robinson, and Felix Guggenheim (whose Pacific Press published the story in a private, "luxury" printing) found themselves butting heads over the copyright. Although contractually bound to Bermann Fischer, and through him to Knopf, Mann had unthinkingly signed over to Robinson the rights to this one story. Lawyers were called in and contentious letters and telegrams criss-crossed the country and the Atlantic. As if this weren't enough, Knopf insisted on having the English version of the story done again from scratch by Mann's regular translator, Helen T. Lowe-Porter, a directive Mann described in his diary as "a terrible blow for Marek," adding, "I am disgusted by these trivialities." He was much less perturbed by a number of critical responses to his story from Jewish commentators who objected to what they perceived as a negative portrayal of the Jews ("the horde"), though he was sorry for what he took to be a misunderstanding of his motivations and a misreading of the piece.

In Robinson's collection, each of the contributions carried as its title one of the commandments; Mann's story, as the first, was given the title "Thou Shalt Have No Other Gods Before Me." Although he explained that his more encompassing German title, *Das Gesetz* (literally, "The Law"), was a designation "not only of the Decalogue, but of moral law as a whole, human civilization itself," Mann himself authorized *The Tables of the Law* for the Lowe-Porter translation. Because of its specificity, as well as its resonance and weight, we have held to this title for our own translation.

If Marek's translation lacks the verve and polish of its source, it is meticulous. The same cannot be said of Lowe-Porter's, of whom Mann's son Golo later wrote, ". . . we always thought [her translations] were very good. Of course, we paid them no attention. Gradually it turned out that they were pretty bad." While her work reads fluently, she tends to simplify Mann's language or omit difficult elements altogether. Furthermore, both earlier translators often employ a now-antiquated vocabulary that may keep a twenty-first-century reader from appreciating the story's Voltaire-inflected humor, whose centrality to his conception Mann stressed again and again (and which he despaired of seeing realized in a translation).

And indeed, the challenges inherent in any translation of a work by Thomas Mann are great. His masterful, perfectly balanced periodic sentences—whose lengthy clauses succeed one another with complete clarity thanks to the German language's rich variety of gendered articles and declined nouns—become unwieldy or obscure in English and must often be divided into smaller units, lightening the character and quickening the pace of the narrative. Mann's style is characterized by the use of leit-motifs, with certain epithets or phrases recurring in an almost Wagnerian manner throughout the text; because no two words have entirely the same range of meaning in both languages, an attempt to preserve these "markers" in translation is another challenge. Mann's frequent use of wordplay and puns, archaic formulations, and neologisms adds to the difficulty. All these stylistic elements create a unique tone, both erudite and arch, dignified and playful, which is an essential component of Mann's identity as a writer. In this new translation, our overarching objective was to be true to this identity.

Mann's noted penchant for paraphrasing other works or even importing passages into his writing was also an issue, for he often incorporates vocabulary, phrases, and sometimes short sections from the Bible in his telling of the Moses story. Where Mann quotes directly from Martin Luther's translation of the Bible, we have used the King James Version as our English-language equivalent.

On March 13, 1943, Mann wrote in his diary: "In the morning I finished the story *Das Gesetz* on the 93rd page. Afterward I corrected the beginnings of the type-script." On March 14: "Thoughts about my old plan for a Novelle on 'Dr. Faust.' Looking around for reading." (One sees why he wrote of his productivity as a narcotic.) *Doctor Faustus* would be the darkest of Mann's major novels, as far as possible from the lightness he strove for in *The Tables of the Law*, whose impassioned conclusion, however, can be read as a kind of modulation to the great, grim work that followed. Indeed, for all its humor and irreverence, Mann's Californian rendering of the ancient Jewish story is informed by the tragedy playing out back in Germany, the dark center of its comic form.

Marion Faber
Stephen Lehmann

THE TABLES
OF THE LAW

ONE

Hɪs ʙɪʀᴛʜ was irregular, and so he passionately loved regularity, the inviolable, commandment and taboo.

As a young man, he had killed in a fiery outburst, and so he knew better than those with no experience that to kill may be sweet, but to have killed is ghastly in the extreme, and that you should not kill.

His senses were hot, and so he yearned for spirituality, purity, and holiness—the invisible, which seemed to him spiritual, holy, and pure.

Because he had killed a man (more about that shortly), he had been forced to flee Egypt, the land of his birth, to live among the Midianites, busy herders and traders dispersed in the desert. There he made the acquaintance of a god whom you could not see, but who saw you; a mountain dweller who at the same time sat invisible upon a portable ark in a tent, where he issued oracles by casting lots. For the children of Midian, this numen, called Yahweh, was one god among many; they did not think much about their duties to him, discharging them only for safety's sake and just in case. It had occurred to them that among the many gods there might possibly be one whom they could not see, a formless one, and they made sacrifices to him only so as to omit nothing, to offend no one, and to avoid unpleasantness from any possible quarter.

Thanks to his longing for purity and holiness, Moses, by contrast, was deeply impressed by Yahweh's invisibility; he believed that no visible god could match an invisible one for holiness, and was amazed that the children of Midian were so quick to dismiss an attribute that to him seemed full of boundless implications. In long, difficult, and vigorous deliberations in the desert while tending the sheep that belonged to the brother of his Midianite wife, shaken by inspirations and revelations, which in one particular case even broke forth from inside him and visited his soul as a flaming external vision, as a literally penetrating revelation and an inescapable mission, he became convinced that Yahweh must be none other than El Elyon, the god most high, El Roi, the god who sees me— the One who has always been called "El Shaddai," "the god of the mountain," El Olam, the god of the world and the everlasting—in a word, none other than the God of Abraham, Isaac, and Jacob, the God of his fathers, that is to say, of the fathers of those tribes back home in the land of Egypt, poor, dark, befuddled in their worship, rootless and enslaved, whose blood on his father's side flowed in his own, in Moses', veins.

For that reason, and filled with this discovery, his soul heavy with its mission but also trembling with the longing to respond to the command, he broke off his sojourn of many years among the children of Midian, set upon an ass his wife Zipporah (a most patrician woman, being a daughter of Reuel, the priest-king in Midian, and the sister of his sheep-owning son Jethro), also taking along his two sons, Gershom and Eliezer, and after a journey of seven days through many deserts, returned west back to the land of Egypt, that is, to the fallow lowlands where the Nile divides and where, in a region called Kessan or sometimes Gesan, Gesem, or Goshen, the blood kin of his father lived and labored.

There he began at once, wherever he walked or stood, in the huts and at the worksites and pasture grounds, to explain to this blood kin his great revelation, dangling his arms in a particular way and shaking his fists tremulously on both sides of his body. He informed them that the God of their fathers had been rediscovered, that He had seen fit to reveal Himself to him, Mosheh ben Amram, at the mountain of Horeb in the wilderness of Sin, from a bush that burned and was not consumed; that His name was Yahweh, which is to be understood as "I am that I am, from everlasting to everlasting," but also as a wafting breeze and a great roar; that He had taken a fancy to their blood kin and was prepared under certain conditions to seal with them a covenant of election from all peoples, assuming, that is, that they would swear allegiance to Him and Him alone and establish a confederacy to serve the Invisible One alone, free of idols.

He goaded them relentlessly with this message, while his fists trembled at the end of his extraordinarily broad wrists. And yet he was not quite honest with them, evading various matters, even the heart of the matter, for fear of unnerving them. He told them nothing, then, of the implications of invisibility, that is of spirituality, purity, and holiness, and preferred not to point out to them that as the sworn servants of the Invisible One they would have to be a people apart, spiritual, pure, and holy. He kept this from them for fear of frightening them; for they were such a miserable, oppressed folk, befuddled in their worship, this blood kin of his father, and he mistrusted them although he loved them. Indeed, when he proclaimed to them that Yahweh, the Invisible One, had taken a fancy to them, he attributed to the god and located in him what might have been the god's, but was also at least in part his own: he himself had taken a fancy to his father's blood kin, as the stone-carver fancies the shapeless block from which he intends to carve a fine, noble shape, the work of his hands—and thus the trembling longing, along with great heaviness of soul at the command, that had suffused him when he set out from Midian.

But what he likewise held back was the second half of the command; for it had been twofold. Not only was he to announce to his tribesmen the rediscovery of the God of their fathers, who fancied them, but he was also to lead them out of the Egyptian house of bondage into the open and through many deserts into the Promised Land, the land of their fathers. This mission was joined to and inextricably intertwined with that of the revelation. God—and liberation for the return home; the Invisible One—and shaking off the yoke of exile: It was one and the same thought for him. But he did not yet tell the people about it, because he knew that the one would follow from the other, and also because he hoped to achieve the second on his own with Pharaoh, the king of Egypt, to whom he was closer than one might think.

Now, whether because his talk displeased the people (for he spoke slowly and haltingly and often could not find his words) or because at the trembling shake of his fists they sensed and marked what was implied by invisibility and by the offer of a covenant (that he wanted to lure them into exhausting and dangerous things), they remained distrustful, stiff-necked, and fearful in the face of his goading. While sneaking a look at their Egyptian taskmasters, they muttered about Moses:

"Why are you going on like this? And what sorts of things are you going on about? Has someone set you above us as our chief or our judge? And who might that be?"

This was nothing new for him. He had heard them say it earlier, before he fled to Midian.

TWO

Hɪs ꜰᴀᴛʜᴇʀ was not his father, nor was his mother his mother—so irregular was his birth. Protected by her guards, the Pharaoh Ramesses' second daughter had been enjoying herself with her ladies-in-waiting in the royal garden by the Nile. There she became aware of a Hebrew laborer who was drawing water, and was overcome with desire for him. He had sad eyes, a bit of fuzz about his chin, and strong arms, visible as he drew the water. He toiled by the sweat of his brow and had his share of troubles, but for Pharaoh's daughter he was a picture of loveliness and desire. She ordered that he be brought to her in her pavilion, and there she ran her exquisite little hand through his sweat-soaked hair, kissed the muscles of his arm, and so teased his manhood that he, the foreign slave, overpowered her, the princess. When they had done, she dismissed him, but he did not go far: after thirty paces he was slain and buried hastily so that nothing remained of the sun-daughter's amusement.

"Poor man," she said when she heard about it. "You guards are always so overeager. He would have kept quiet.

He loved me." But then she became pregnant and after nine months gave birth in all secrecy to a boy whom her maidens laid in an ark of pitch and bulrushes and hid in the reeds at the edge of the water. They found it later and called out: "O wonder, a foundling, a boy of the reeds, an abandoned baby! It is just as in the old tales, as with Sargon, whom Akki, the drawer of water, found in the rushes and raised in the kindness of his heart. Such things happen again and again! Now, where shall we take this discovery? The very most sensible thing would be to give him to a nursing mother of humble estate, one with extra milk so that he may grow up as her son and her honest husband's." And they handed the child over to a Hebrew woman who brought him down to the region of Goshen, to Jochebed, the wife of Amram, one of the Hebrew immigrants, a member of Levi's tribe. She was nursing her son Aaron and had extra milk; therefore, and because from time to time good things came secretly to her household from above, she raised the mysterious child, too, in the kindness of her heart.

Thus Amram and Jochebed became known as his parents, and Aaron was his brother. Amram possessed cattle and land, and Jochebed was the daughter of a stone-carver. But they did not know what they should call the problematic little boy; and they therefore gave him a half-Egyptian name, that is to say, half of an Egyptian name. For the sons of the land were often called Ptah-Moses,

Amen-Moses, or Ra-Moses, named as the sons of their gods. Amram and Jochebed, however, preferred to leave out the name of a god, and called the boy Moses, pure and simple. So he was quite simply a "son." But the question remained, "Whose?"

THREE

He grew up as one of the immigrants and spoke in their dialect. Once, during a period of drought, frontier officials had given the ancestors of this blood kin permission to come into the land as "starving Bedouins of Edom," as Pharaoh's scribes called them, and they had been assigned the district of Goshen in the lowlands for use as grazing land. Anyone who thinks they were allowed to graze there for free does not know much about their hosts, the children of Egypt. Not only did they have to give some of their cattle in taxes, and so many that it hurt, but everyone with any strength had to do work as well, enforced labor in the various projects which, in a land like Egypt, are always being built. But it was especially after Ramesses, the second of his name, became Pharaoh in Thebes that the building became excessive—it was his pleasure and his royal delight. He built extravagant temples throughout the land, and down by the estuaries he not only renewed and very much improved the long-neglected canal which connected the eastern arm of the Nile with the Bitter Lakes, thus joining the great sea with the tip of the Red Sea, but along the course of the canal he also erected two whole treasure-cities, called Pithom and Raamses, and for these the children of the immigrants, the Ibrim, were called upon to bake and tow bricks, and slave by the sweat of their bodies under the Egyptian rod.

In truth, this rod was merely the emblem of Pharaoh's overseers; the Ibrim were not beaten with it unnecessarily. They also had enough to eat while they labored: plentiful fish from the Nile, bread, beer, and beef, as much as they needed. Nevertheless, it could not be said that the labor suited or appealed to them, for they were of a nomadic blood, with the tradition of a free, wandering life, and for them, working regular hours, being made to sweat, was deeply alien and annoying. But these tribes were affiliated too loosely and were not sufficiently aware of themselves to agree on and be of one mind about their displeasure. Because they had camped for several generations in a transit land between the home of their fathers and Egypt proper, their soul was formless, with a spirit that wavered, and without a firm doctrine; they had forgotten much, had half-learned new things, and because they lacked a true center, they did not trust their own feelings, not even the anger fueled by their servitude, for the fish, beer, and beef addled their brains.

When Moses, allegedly the son of Amram, outgrew his youthful years, he would have had to make bricks for Pharaoh, too. But that did not happen; instead the youth was taken from his parents and brought to a school in Upper Egypt, a very refined boarding school where the sons of Syrian lords were educated along with scions of the local nobility. That is where he was placed, for his natural mother, Pharaoh's child, who had delivered him into the reeds, a lecherous creature, to be sure, but not without a heart, had thought of him in consideration of his hastily buried father, the water-drawer with the bit of fuzz and sad eyes, and she did not want him to remain among the savages, but to be educated as an Egyptian and to attain a position at the court, in secret semi-recognition of his divine semi-nobility. So Moses, dressed in white linen and with a wig upon his head, learned astronomy and geography, calligraphy and law, although he was not really happy among the dandies of the elegant boarding school, but kept to himself, repelled by the Egyptian gentility and its pleasures, which had given birth to him. The blood of the hastily buried man who had served this pleasure was stronger in him than the Egyptian portion, and in his heart he was true to the poor, formless souls at home in Goshen, who did not have the courage of their anger. He was true to them in the face of the lecherous arrogance of his mother's blood.

"What is your name again?" the comrades at school would ask him.

"I'm called Moses," he would answer.

"Ach-Moses or Ptah-Moses?" they asked.

"No, just Moses," he replied.

"That's pathetic and weird," said the snooty boys, and he grew so angry he would have liked to slay them and give them a hasty burial. For he understood that such questions were meant only to pry into his irregular birth, whose wavering outlines everyone already knew. That he was nothing but the secret fruit of Egyptian pleasure not even he would have known had it not been common knowledge, however vague—known all the way up to Pharaoh, who had been left as little in the dark about his child's coquetry as Moses was about the fact that contemptible, murderous pleasure had turned Ramesses, the builder, into his lechery-grandfather. Yes, Moses knew this and also knew that Pharaoh knew it, and at that thought he nodded his head threateningly in the direction of Pharaoh's throne.

THOMAS MANN

FOUR

Aᶠᵗᵉʳ ʜᵉ had lived for two years among the fops at the Theban school, he could stand it no longer. He made his escape over the wall by night and wandered home to his father's blood kin in Goshen. With a bitter face he roamed among them, and one day along the canal near Ramesses' new buildings he saw an Egyptian overseer take his rod and beat one of the laborers, who had probably been negligent or contrary. Turning pale and with fiery eyes, he challenged the Egyptian who, instead of giving him any kind of answer, punched in the bridge of his nose, so that for the rest of his life it had a broken, flatly indented bone. But Moses seized the rod from the overseer, took a mighty swing and crushed the man's skull, killing him on the spot. He hadn't even looked around to see whether anyone was watching. But it was a desolate place and no one else was nearby. So he hastily buried the slain man quite on his own, for the fellow he had defended had taken to the hills; and it seemed to him that he'd always had it in mind to slay somebody and bury him hastily.

His fiery deed remained hidden, at least from the Egyptians, who never found out why their man had not turned up, and days and years passed over the deed. Moses continued to roam among his father's people and meddled in their disputes with a strange highhandedness. One time he saw two Ibrim laborers quarreling with one another, on the brink of coming to blows. "Why are you quarreling and even about to fight?" he said to them. "Haven't you sunk low enough? Shouldn't you stand by your own kind instead of baring your teeth at one another? That one is in the wrong, I saw it. He should give in and be still, and the other one shouldn't lord it over him."

But as soon as he had finished speaking, the two of them were suddenly united against him, saying, "Why are you interfering in our affairs?" The one who had been found at fault was especially snotty and said quite loudly, "That's the absolute limit! Who are you to go sticking your goat-nose into things that don't concern you? Oh yes, that's right, you're Mosheh, the son of Amram, but that's not saying much and nobody really knows who you are, not even you. We'd like to know who appointed you over us as our judge and master. Maybe you'd like to strangle me, too, the way you strangled the Egyptian that time and buried him hastily?"

"Be quiet!" said Moses, appalled, and he thought, How has that gotten around? On the very same day he realized that this country could no longer be his dwelling place, and he crossed the border where it was not secured, through the mudflats near the Bitter Seas. He wandered through many deserts of the land of Sinai and came to Midian, to the Midianites and their priest-king, Reuel.

FIVE

WHEN HE returned to Egypt, filled with his discovery of God and his mission, he was a man in his prime, sturdy, with a flat nose, prominent cheekbones, a parted beard, wide-set eyes, and broad wrists—which were especially obvious when, as frequently happened, he was brooding and covered his mouth and beard with his right hand. From hut to hut and from labor site to labor site he went, and shaking his fists by his thighs he spoke of the Invisible One, the God of his fathers, who was prepared to enter into a covenant. For all intents and purposes, however, he could not speak, for he was essentially bottled up by nature, and when agitated was inclined to have a thick tongue. Furthermore, he wasn't really at home in any language and when speaking would cast about in three: Aramaic Syro-Chaldean, which his father's blood kin spoke and which he had learned from his parents, had been overlaid by Egyptian, which he had had to acquire at school, and in addition Midianite Arabic, which he had spoken for many years in the desert. So he was always jumbling them up.

Most helpful to him was his brother, Aaron, a rangy, gentle man with a black beard and black ringlets down his neck, who liked to keep his large, rounded eyelids piously lowered. Moses had initiated him into everything, had completely won him over to the idea of the Invisible One and all its implications, and since Aaron was able to speak through his beard with unctuous fluency, he usually accompanied Moses on his recruitment rounds and spoke in his stead, in a drawling, oily manner, to be sure, and not emphatically enough, so that Moses would try with shaking fists to put more fire into his words and often interrupted him, higgledy-piggledy, in Aramaic-Egyptian-Arabic.

Aaron's wife was named Elisheba, the daughter of Amminadab; she too was party to the vow and the propaganda, as was Miriam, a younger sister of Moses and Aaron, an ardent woman who could sing and play the timbrel. But Moses was especially fond of a young man who, for his part, was devoted heart and soul to him, his revelation, and his plans, and never left his side. He was actually named Hosea, the son of Nun (which means "fish") of Ephraim's clan. But Moses had given him the Yahweh-name of Yehoshua, also shortened to Joshua, and he bore that name with pride—a straight-backed, wiry young man with a head of woolly hair, a prominent Adam's apple, and a pair of particularly deep furrows between his eyebrows, who had his own point of view about the whole thing, not the religious point of view so much as the military. Yahweh, the God of his fathers, was for Joshua the God of hosts above all else, and in his mind the thought of escape out of the house of bondage, which was inextricably linked with God's name, was combined with the conquest of new settlement areas of their own for the Hebrew tribes—which was logical, because they had to live somewhere, and no land, promised or not, would just be handed over to them.

Joshua, as young as he was, carried all the pertinent facts in his woolly head, with its firm, steady gaze, and he incessantly discussed them with Moses, his older friend and master. Without having the wherewithal for an accurate census, he had estimated that the strength of the clans camping in Goshen and residing in the storage-cities Pithom and Raamses, as well as those clan members scattered over the rest of the land as slaves, came to approximately twelve or thirteen thousand head, all in all, which would constitute a weapons-ready force of approximately three thousand. Later the numbers were wildly exaggerated, but Joshua was more or less right about them, and they didn't suit him at all. Three thousand men was not a particularly terrifying army, not even if you assumed that once you were on your way all sorts of related blood kin who were wandering around in the desert would join this nucleus to conquer the land. You couldn't contemplate a serious undertaking based solely on a force of this size; to rely on it to strike into the Promised Land would be ill advised. Joshua understood that, and for that reason he was trying to find a place out in the open where the blood kin could first establish themselves—and where under reasonably favorable circumstances they could be left to grow at their natural rate for a while, which, if Joshua knew his people, came to two and one half per hundred each year. The young man kept his eye out for a place where they could preserve and propagate themselves to increase their armed force, and he often consulted with Moses about this, revealing in the process that he had a surprisingly clear grasp of how one place related to another in the world, keeping in his head a kind of map of potential tracts of land according to their sizes, daylong marches, and watering holes, and especially the bellicosity of their inhabitants.

Moses knew what he had in his Joshua, knew well that he would have need of him, and loved his intentness, although its immediate objects did not concern him much. Covering mouth and beard with his right hand, he listened to the young man's strategic pronouncements and thought of other things. Of course, Moses, too, thought of Yahweh in connection with an exodus—but not simply a military campaign to conquer land, rather an exodus into open land and into apartness. It meant that somewhere out there in the open he would have for himself all this mass of bewildered flesh wavering among various traditions, these procreating men, lactating women, impulsive youths, snotty-nosed children, the blood kin of his father; that he would inculcate them with the holy-invisible God, the pure, the spiritual one; that he could set up this God as their collective, formative center and shape them in His image. They would be a people different from all others, belonging to God, a people formed and defined by what is holy and spiritual, distinguished from all others by their dread, forbearance, awe, that is to say, by their fear of the thought of purity, by a code of restraint which, since the Invisible One was actually God of the whole world, would bind all people together in the future, but was first to be decreed for them and their austere privilege among the heathens.

This was Moses' fancy for his father's blood kin, his fancy as a creator, which for him was at one with the benevolent choice God had made and His willingness to enter into a covenant. Since he believed that the formation in God's image had to take precedence over all other ventures that the young Joshua had in mind, and furthermore that this required time, free time out in open land—he did not mind that there was still a hitch in Joshua's plans and that they were stymied by the inadequate number of weapons-ready men. Joshua needed time so that the people could increase by natural means—and also, by the way, so that he, himself, could grow older and be permitted to appoint himself their commander; and Moses needed time for the work of creating, which he desired in the name of God. And so while holding differing viewpoints, they were in agreement.

SIX

Meanwhile, however, God's emissary, along with his closest disciples, the eloquent Aaron, Elisheba, Miriam, Joshua, and one Caleb, who was the same age as Joshua and his bosom friend, another strong, simple, brave young man—meanwhile not one of them wasted a single day in spreading among their own the message of Yahweh, the Invisible One and His flattering offer of a covenant, while simultaneously fueling the bitterness at their work under the Egyptian rod and raising the idea that they should shake off this yoke and emigrate. Each one did it in his own way: Moses himself with halting words and shaking fists, Aaron in drawling, fluent discourse, Elisheba with wheedling chatter, Joshua and Caleb like military commanders, in clipped slogans; Miriam, who was soon called "the prophetess," did it in a loftier tone, to timbrel accompaniment. Nor did their sermons fall upon hard ground; the thought of swearing allegiance to Moses' covenant-fancying God, of dedicating themselves to the Imageless One as His people and of migrating under Him and His spokesman into open land, took root among the tribes

and began to form their unifying center—this was especially so because Moses promised, or rather offered the
hope-filled expectation, that he would negotiate with
the most powerful authorities permission for them all to
leave Egypt so that it would not have to take the form of a
risky uprising, but rather could follow upon an amicable
agreement. They were familiar, if only vaguely, with his
half-Egyptian birth into the reeds; they knew about the
elegant education he'd enjoyed for a while and the dark
relationship that he commanded with the court. What
once had been a reason to mistrust and reject him, that is,
his mixed blood and that he had one foot in Egyptian life,
was now transformed into a source of trust and lent him
authority. Certainly, if anybody could, he was the man to
stand before Pharaoh and argue their case. And so they
commissioned him to try to persuade Ramesses, builder
and slavemaster, to release them—and not just Moses,
but also his milk-brother, Aaron, for Moses intended to
take him along, first because he himself could not speak
coherently and Aaron could, and also because Aaron was
accomplished in certain sleights-of-hand, which they
hoped would make an impression at court to the glory
of Yahweh. He could make a cobra stiff as a rod by press-
ing on its neck; but if he then cast the rod to the ground,
it would curl and "transform itself into a serpent." Neither Moses nor Aaron anticipated the fact that Pharaoh's
magicians were also familiar with this miracle and that it

would therefore not be able to serve as terrifying proof of Yahweh's power.

They had no luck whatsoever—let's say it at once—no matter how cunningly they presented the case they'd put together with young Joshua and Caleb and the war council. They had decided to ask the king only for permission for the Hebrew people to travel three days' distance beyond the border out into the desert to celebrate a sacrifice to the Lord their God who had called them, and then return to work. They hardly expected Pharaoh to be taken in by this feint and believe that they would return. It was only a gentler, more courteous form of submitting a plea for emancipation, but it didn't earn them any gratitude from the king.

The brothers did succeed, however, in actually getting into the Great House and in front of Pharaoh's throne, and not merely once, but through doggedly persistent negotiations over and over again. In this respect Moses had not promised his people too much, for he was counting on the fact that Ramesses was his secret lechery-grandfather and that each of them knew that the other knew it. It enabled Moses to put a great deal of pressure on the king, and even though it was never enough to wring from him his consent to their exodus, it did make Moses a serious negotiator and gained him repeated access to the powerful man, who feared him. A king's fear is dangerous, of course, and all this time Moses was playing a risky game.

He was brave—how brave he was and what an impression he made on his people, we shall see very soon. It would have been easy for Ramesses to have him strangled quietly and hastily buried, so that in the end really nothing would be left of his child's sensual whim. But the princess retained a sweet memory of that little hour and did not want any harm to come to her boy of the reeds—he stood under her protection, however ungratefully he responded to her efforts on his behalf, her plans for his education and promotion.

So Moses and Aaron were permitted to stand before Pharaoh, but he roundly denied their request for a sacrificial holiday out in open land to which their God had allegedly called their people. It was no use that Aaron spoke with unctuous coherence while Moses passionately shook his fists by his thighs. Nor did it help that Aaron turned his rod into a serpent, for Pharaoh's magicians did the same thing on the spot, thereby proving that the Invisible One, in Whose name the two were speaking, ought to be accorded no remarkable powers and that Pharaoh didn't have to listen to the voice of this Lord. "If we don't make a three days' journey into the wilderness and prepare a feast for the Lord, our tribes will be visited by pestilence or the sword," said the brothers. But the king answered, "That does not concern us. You are numerous enough, more than twelve thousand strong, and you can certainly bear some reduction, whether through pestilence or the sword or harsh work. You, Moses and Aaron, you only want to indulge your people in idleness and give them respite from the service they owe me. I cannot tolerate that and will not allow it. I have several fabulous temples in the works, and I also want to build a third treasure-city besides Pithom and Raamses, to add to those two, and for that I need the arms of your people. I thank you for your ably-presented proposal, and you, Moses, I even dismiss you in special favor, willy-nilly. But no more talk of holidays in the desert!"

Thus was the audience terminated and not only did nothing good come of it, but definite evil came of it afterward. For Pharaoh, offended in his hunger for buildings and annoyed that he could not very well strangle Moses—because if he did his daughter would make a scene—ordered that the Goshen-people be given a workload even harsher than before and that they not be spared the rod if they were slack; let them have plenty to do, so that they would work until they dropped and all their idle thoughts of desert festivals for their god would disappear. And that's what happened. Because Moses and Aaron had spoken before Pharaoh, the labor grew harsher from one day to the next. No longer did the people receive delivery of the straw to be burned in their bricks, for example; now they had to go to the stubble-fields themselves to gather the necessary straw. Yet the number of bricks to be manufactured was not reduced for that reason; the same quota had to be filled or else the rod would dance on the poor men's backs. In vain did the Hebrew foremen supervising the people complain to the authorities about unreasonable demands. The answer was, "You're idle, idle is what you are, and that's why you cry out and say, 'We want to leave here and celebrate a sacrifice.' But the order stands: you'll keep getting the straw yourselves and you'll keep making the same number of bricks."

SEVEN

FOR MOSES and Aaron, this was no small embarrass-
ment. The foremen said to them, "There you have it!
That's our reward for the covenant with your God and
for Moses' connections. All you've done is taint us in the
presence of Pharaoh and his men, and put the sword into
their hands to destroy us."

There was not much to be said in response, and
Moses had some difficult private hours with the God of
the burning bush as he admonished Him that he, Moses,
had been dead set against taking on this mission from the
start, that he had asked Him right off to send anyone else,
just not him, since he was so inarticulate. But the Lord
had answered him that Aaron, after all, was eloquent.
Yes, of course, he had done the talking, but in much too
oily a manner, and it just went to show how preposter-
ous it was to take on a cause if you yourself have a thick
tongue and have to let other people step in and speak
for you. But from within him, the God comforted and
rebuked him and answered that he should be ashamed
of his faint heart; his excuses were pure affectation, for

at bottom he himself had been itching for the call, since he fancied his people and a chance to shape them just as much as the God did, in fact, and you couldn't really distinguish his own fancy from that of the God's at all, rather it was at one with it: it was a god's fancy that had driven him to the task, and he should be ashamed to lose heart at the first defeat.

Moses accepted this, and all the more because in the war council with Joshua, Caleb, Aaron, and the ardent women, they had concluded that the increased oppression, however much bad blood it might generate, was upon closer inspection not such a terrible first result; for it was creating bad blood not only toward Moses but above all toward the Egyptians, and it would make the people all the more receptive to the call of the Savior-God and the thought of an exodus into open land. And thus it was; the agitation about the straw and bricks grew among the laborers, and the reproach that Moses had tainted them and done them nothing but harm receded behind the wish that Amram's son might exploit his connections again and go once more to Pharaoh for their sake.

And that he did, this time not with Aaron, but alone, whatever his tongue might do; he shook his fists before the throne and demanded in halting, blurted words the exodus of his people into the open, under the name of a sacrificial festival in the desert. And he did this, not *one* time only, but maybe even ten, for Moses' connections were so good that Pharaoh could not very well deny him access to his throne. There unfolded a struggle, dogged and protracted, between him and the king, never leading, it is true, to the latter's agreeing to Moses' demand, but instead to one fine day when, rather than releasing them, the Egyptians pushed and drove the Goshen-people out of their land, just glad in the end to be rid of them.

About this struggle and the pressure exerted on the stubbornly resistant king during the course of it, there has been much chatter, not without some historical underpinnings, but strongly characterized by embellishment. There's talk of the ten plagues that Yahweh visited upon the Egyptians one after the other in order to wear Pharaoh down, while at the same time intentionally hardening Pharaoh's heart against Moses' appeal, so that He would have a chance to demonstrate His power with ever new plagues. Blood, frogs, vermin, wild animals, boils, pestilence, hail, locusts, darkness, and death of the firstborn—those were the ten plagues, and none of them would be impossible; but it is an open question whether, with the exception of the last one (which was an especially obscure case, never really cleared up), they significantly affected the final outcome. There are conditions under which the Nile takes on a blood-red color, its water becomes temporarily undrinkable, and the fish die. Such things happen, just as the frogs of the swamp disproportionately increase in number, or the ever-present lice propagate to a level that would approach an infestation. And there were still a lot of lions around, too, roaming at the edge of the desert and lurking in the jungles by the dried-up river channels, and if the number of rapacious attacks on man and beast increased, you could go ahead and call it a plague. And aren't scabies and boils common in the land of Egypt, and how easily might not evil blains rise up out of uncleanliness and fester as pestilence among the people? The sky is usually blue in those parts, and thus all the more deep an impression would a rare violent thunderstorm make, when fire descending from the clouds combines with dense pebbles of hail, pounding the crops and thrashing the trees, even if it were not connected to a particular intent. Locusts are all-too-familiar guests, and mankind has invented various means of scaring and warding them off when they approach en masse, although their ravenousness does win out in the end, so that entire fields are reduced to gnawed-down baldness. And anyone who has ever experienced the anxious, gloomy mood spread over the earth by a cosmically shaded sun will understand quite well that a people pampered by light would give such an eclipse the name "plague."

And with that the number of reported evils is at an end, for the tenth one, the death of the firstborn, does not actually belong in this count but constitutes an ambiguous by-product of the exodus itself, uncanny in its details. Perhaps only some of the other ones happened or—distributed over a longer period of time—perhaps all of them: we really must consider their names as nothing more than embroidered circumlocutions for the one single pressure that Moses always used against Ramesses, that is, the fact that Pharaoh was his lechery-grandfather and that Moses was in a position to broadcast this around. More than once, the king was about to cave in to this pressure; at the least, he made great concessions. He would permit the men to leave for the sacrificial festival, but the women, children, and herds would have to remain behind. Moses did not accept that: young and old, sons and daughters, sheep and cattle, all must leave, for this concerned a festival for the Lord. Then Pharaoh would permit women and offspring, too, excluding only the livestock, which was to remain behind as collateral. But where, Moses demanded, were they to get their butchered and burnt offerings for the festival if they didn't have their livestock with them? Not one hoof could stay behind, he insisted—which made it very clear he wasn't talking about a holiday, but an exodus.

The hooves resulted in a last stormy scene between the Egyptian majesty and Yahweh's emissary. During the whole negotiation, Moses had shown great patience, but fist-shaking choler also lay within his nature. Finally Pharaoh reached his limit and literally chased him from the room. "Out!" he cried, "And take care that you never come before me again. Otherwise it will mean your death," whereupon Moses, who was still very agitated, grew completely calm and answered simply, "You have spoken. I am going and will not come before you again." As he took his leave with such fearful serenity, his thoughts turned to things that were not really to his liking. They were, however, to the liking of young Joshua and Caleb.

EIGHT

Tʜɪꜱ ɪꜱ a dark chapter, which can only be related in fragmented, veiled phrases. There came a day, or rather, a night, a grim vesper hour, when Yahweh went about, or his angel of death did, and visited the tenth plague upon the children of Egypt, or rather a portion of them, the Egyptian element among the inhabitants of Goshen as well as of the cities of Pithom and Raamses, while omitting and sparing those huts and houses whose doorposts were smeared with blood as a signal.

What did he do? He set in motion a dying, the dying of the firstborn among the Egyptian element, and by doing so he fulfilled many a secret wish and helped many a second-born to come into his own, something that would otherwise have been denied him. Please note the distinction between Yahweh and his angel of death: it establishes that it was not Yahweh himself who went about, but in fact his angel of death—more precisely, a carefully chosen host of angels. If, however, you want to reduce them to a single manifestation, there is good reason to think of Yahweh's angel of death as a straight-backed figure of a youth with a head of woolly hair, a prominent Adam's apple, and deep furrows between his eyebrows, an angel from that strain that always rejoices when you've put an end to useless negotiations and can proceed to action.

There had been no lack of preparations for decisive acts during Moses' tenacious negotiations with Pharaoh: as for Moses himself, they had been confined to his secretly sending his wife and sons back to Midian, to his brother-in-law Jethro, in anticipation of difficult events to come, so as not to be burdened with worries about them. But Joshua, whose relationship to Moses was unmistakably similar to that of the angel of death to Yahweh, had acted in his own fashion, and since he did not possess the means nor yet the reputation to mobilize under his command those three thousand able-bodied blood-comrades, he had at least selected a squad from them, had armed, drilled, and disciplined them so that they could achieve something from the start.

What happened then is shrouded in darkness—in the darkness of that vesper night that the children of Egypt saw as a night of celebration for the laboring slaves who lived among them. It seemed that these slaves wanted to make up for the vetoed sacrificial festival in the desert with a lantern festival to their god, complete with banquet, right here at home, and they had even borrowed gold and silver vessels for it from their Egyptian neighbors. However, combined with this event, or rather, instead of it, that angel of death went about, and in every domicile that a bundle of hyssop had not smeared with blood, the firstborn died. This visitation brought with it such great confusion, such a sudden reversal of the relationships of law and entitlement, that from one hour to the next the road out of the land not only stood open for Moses' people, but they were virtually forced onto it and couldn't take it quickly enough to suit the Egyptians. It actually does seem that the second-born were less eager to avenge the death of those whose place they took than they were to urge the people who caused their elevation to clear out.

According to tradition, this tenth plague had finally broken Pharaoh's pride so that he had released the blood kin of Moses' father from their bondage. He did, however, promptly send a division of his army in pursuit of the escapees, though it miraculously came to a bad end.

Be that as it may, the emigration took on the form of an expulsion, and the haste with which this happened is recorded in this detail: No one had time to leaven the bread for the journey; they could provide only those flat cakes of affliction that Moses afterward turned into a commemorative celebratory custom for all time. For the rest, all of them, big and small, had been completely ready to set out. Even as the angel of death went about, they had sat next to their loaded carts, their loins girded, their shoes already on their feet, their walking-staffs in their hands. They brought along the gold and silver vessels they had borrowed from the locals.

My friends! At the exodus out of Egypt there was both killing and stealing. But according to Moses' firm will, it was to be for the last time. How should man wrest himself from impurity without making one last sacrifice to it and polluting himself thoroughly in the process? Moses now had the incarnate object of his creative fancy, this formless humankind, his father's blood kin, free in open land, and freedom for him was the realm of sanctification.

NINE

THE WANDERING mass of people—far fewer in its head-count than what legend would claim, but difficult enough to manage, to control, and to feed, a sufficiently heavy burden on the shoulders of the man responsible for their fate, for their survival out in the open—took the route that automatically presented itself if (for good reason) they were to avoid the fortifications that began on the Egyptian border, north of the Bitter Seas. This route led through the region of the salt seas into which the larger, westernmost arm of the Red Sea flows, shaping the land of the Sinai into a peninsula. Moses knew this territory, having passed through it on his flight into Midian and his return thence. More than the young Joshua, whose only map was a mental one, Moses was familiar with its contours, the nature of those reedy mudflats, which at times formed the Bitter Seas' open connection to the gulf and through which, under certain conditions, one could reach the land of Sinai dry-shod. For if a strong east wind was blowing and the seas were driven back, the mudflats offered open passage—and thanks to Yahweh's favorable disposition, this was the condition of the Sea of Reeds when the fugitives came upon it.

It was Joshua and Caleb who spread the word among the throng that Moses, invoking God, had held his rod over the waters, causing them to part and present a clear way for the people. And Moses probably had done that, had aided the east wind with his ceremonial gesture in Yahweh's name. In any case, the people's belief in their leader was all the more in need of strengthening at this particular juncture, because just here, here first of all, it was put to a difficult test. For it was here that Pharaoh's military, men and chariots, terrible scythed chariots, which they knew only too well, caught up to the emigrants and came within a hair's breadth of putting a bloody end to their journey toward God.

The news of this approach, announced by Joshua's rear guard, aroused extreme terror and wild despair in the people. Their regret at having followed "this man Moses" promptly flared up into a bright blaze, triggering that mass grumbling which, to Moses' grief and bitterness, was to recur at every difficulty they encountered. The women wailed; the men cursed and shook their fists by their thighs just the way Moses did when he was agitated. "Were there not graves in Egypt," they said, "where we could have gone peacefully when our hour came, if we had stayed at home?" All of a sudden, Egypt was "home," where it had used to be an exile of enforced labor. "Better for us to have served the Egyptians than to die by the sword in the wilderness!" Moses heard this a thousand times, and it even embittered him about their rescue, which turned out to be overwhelming. He was "the man Moses, who led us out of Egypt"—which meant shouts of praise as long as everything was going well. But if things went badly, it quickly took on a different tone and meant a grumbling reproach that was never very far from the thought of a stoning.

Then, after a short period of alarm, things took an embarrassingly and unbelievably good turn. Moses stood there, very regal through divine miracle, and was "the man, who led us out of Egypt"—now meant the other way round again. The blood kin push through the drained mudflats, the Egyptian army chasing behind them in their chariots. Suddenly the wind dies down, the tide returns, and men and steeds perish gurgling in the engulfing waters.

It was an unparalleled triumph. Miriam, the prophetess, Aaron's sister, sang to her timbrel, leading the women in their singing and dancing: "Sing unto the Lord—a glorious deed—the horse and his rider—hath He thrown into the sea." She had written this herself. You must imagine it sung to timbrel accompaniment.

The people were deeply moved. The words "mighty," "holy," "terrifying," "admirable," and "miracle-working" issued endlessly from their lips, and it was unclear whether they were intended for the godhead or for Moses, God's head man, whose rod, they assumed, had brought the drowning floodwaters down upon Egypt's forces. It was easy to get the two confused. Whenever the people weren't grumbling about him, Moses always had his hands full trying to keep them from thinking that he himself was a god, the One he was proclaiming.

TEN

AND REALLY that wasn't so ridiculous, for what he was beginning to expect of these poor souls went far beyond the human norm and could hardly have originated in the mind of a mortal. It made your jaw drop to think about it. After Miriam's singing and dancing, he immediately forbade any further rejoicing at the Egyptians' demise. He proclaimed: Even Yahweh's heavenly armies had been about to join in the victory song, but the Holy One rebuked them—"What's this? My creatures drown in the sea and you want to sing?" He spread this short, but astonishing story around and added, "Thou shalt not rejoice at the fall of thine enemy; let not your heart be glad at his misfortune." It was the first time that the entire horde, twelve thousand and a few hundred head of them, including the three thousand able-bodied men, had been appealed to with "thou," that form of address which encompassed their totality and at the same time trained an eye on each of them, man and woman, young and old, as if poking a finger in the chest of every one. "Thou shalt raise no cries of joy at the fall of thine enemy." That was positively unnatural! But obviously this unnaturalness was connected to the invisibility of Moses' God, who wanted to be their God. It began to dawn on the more alert members of the brown horde what that meant and how mysterious and challenging it was to have sworn allegiance to an invisible god.

They were in the land of Sinai, more precisely in the wilderness of Shur, an unfriendly terrain that they would leave only to arrive in another just as lamentable—the wilderness of Paran. Why these wildernesses had different names is a mystery; they abutted one another in their aridness, the same accursed rocky fields, without water or vegetation, extending in a line of dead hills as long as three days' journey, and even four and five. It was a good thing that Moses had so quickly infused the respect accorded him at the Sea of Reeds with that supernatural dimension, for now all of a sudden he was again "this man Moses who led us out of Egypt," which meant "who brought misfortune upon us," and a loud grumbling assaulted his ears. After three days, the water they had brought became a trickle. Thousands were thirsting, the relentless sun on their heads and under their feet the barren desolation of the wilderness of Shur—if it wasn't by now the wilderness of Paran. "What are we to drink?" they cried aloud, showing no sensitivity to the suffering of their leader under the weight of his responsibility. He wished that he alone would drink nothing, never again have anything to drink, if only *they* might have something so that he didn't have to hear their "Why did you make us leave Egypt?" To suffer alone is small agony compared with that of having to answer for such a horde, and Moses was a very burdened man, and stayed that way ever after, burdened above all men on earth.

Very soon there wasn't anything left to eat either, for how long could the hastily packed flatbread hold out? "What are we to eat?" This cry resounded now, too, sobbing and scolding, and Moses had some difficult private hours with God, when he admonished Him for His harshness in having laid the burden of this entire people upon him, His servant. "Am I the one who conceived and bore all these people," he asked, "so that you say to me, 'Carry them in your arms!' Where am I to get the food to give all these people? They are weeping before me and saying, 'Give us meat so that we can eat!' I cannot carry so many alone. It is too hard for me. And if that's the way You want to treat me, please strangle me instead so that I do not have to witness my misfortune and theirs!"

And Yahweh did not leave him completely in the lurch. As for water, on the fifth day, while crossing a high plateau, they spotted a tree-lined spring, which, by the way, was also marked as the Spring of Marah on the map that Joshua carried in his head. Its water tasted foul, it's true, due to unpleasant admixtures, eliciting bitter disappointment and great waves of grumbling. But

Moses, made inventive by necessity, applied a kind of filtering device that kept back the nasty impurities, if not entirely, at least in good measure, and so performed a kind of spring-miracle, transforming the outcries into cheers and greatly helping to restore his reputation. The phrase "who led us out of Egypt" once again took on a rosy connotation.

As for food, there occurred yet another miracle, which at first triggered joyful amazement. For it turned out that large areas of the wilderness of Paran were covered with lichen that one could eat, manna-lichen, a sugary, felt-like substance, round and small, like coriander seeds in appearance and like bdellium in color. It spoiled quickly and began to smell bad if it wasn't eaten right away, but otherwise—ground, beaten, or prepared as ashcakes—it was quite tolerable in a pinch, tasting almost like wafers with honey, some people said, and others said, like oil-cake.

That was the first, positive judgment, but it didn't last. Soon, even after just a few days, the people had had enough of the manna and were tired of filling up on it. As their only nourishment, it quickly became repugnant and nauseated them, so that they complained: "We're remembering the fish that we could eat for free in Egypt, the pumpkins, marrow squash, leeks, onions, and garlic. But now our souls are weary, for our eyes see nothing but manna."

That's what Moses heard to his pain, along with the predictable question: "Why did you make us leave Egypt?" What he asked God was, "What should I do with these people? They don't want to eat manna anymore. Just wait, You'll see. Before long they'll be stoning me."

ELEVEN

H_E WAS more or less protected from that fate, thanks to his disciple Yehoshua and the armed squad he had gathered together in Goshen, which surrounded the liberator as soon as any threatening grumbles erupted among the rabble. For the moment, it was a small squad of young men, with Caleb as lieutenant, but Joshua was just waiting for an opportunity to establish himself as commander and champion, in order to direct all the able-bodied men, all three thousand of them, according to his will. And he knew that this opportunity was imminent.

Moses greatly valued the young man whom he had designated with the name of God; without him, he would sometimes have been quite lost. Moses was a spiritual man, and his manliness, sturdy and strong as it was, with his wrists as broad as a stone-carver's, was spiritual, an introverted manliness, restrained and fiercely fired up by God, removed from the world, concerned only with the holy. With a kind of blitheness that contrasted strangely with his usual brooding meditations, when he covered his mouth and beard with his hand, he had confined all his thoughts and deeds to setting his father's blood kin apart for himself alone, in order to shape it and to carve unhindered a holy image of God out of the hopeless mass that he loved. He had worried not at all, or only a little, about the dangers of freedom, the difficulties of the desert, or the question of how so many rabble were to be brought through it intact, or even about where to take those people. And he was in no way prepared for practical leadership. So he could only be grateful to have Joshua at his side, who for his part revered the spiritual manliness in Moses and unreservedly put his own straight-backed, utterly extroverted, youthful manliness at his disposal.

It was thanks to Joshua that they actually set forth in the desert with a firm objective and didn't wear themselves out in aimless wandering. He determined the direction for their march by the stars, calculated the daylong marches, and took care that they would reach the watering places in bearable, if sometimes only just bearable, intervals. It was he who had figured out that they could eat the round lichen. In a word, he protected his master's reputation as a leader and saw to it that the phrase "who led us out of Egypt," whenever it had become a grumbling, took on its laudatory sense again. He had the destination clearly in his head, and guided by the stars, in agreement with Moses, he steered toward it by the shortest way possible. For the two concurred about needing a first destination, a fixed if also temporary accommodation, a dwelling place where they could live comfortably and gain some time, in fact much time: partly (in Joshua's mind) so that the people could multiply and provide him as he matured with a greater number of able-bodied forces, partly (in Moses' mind) so that he could, above all, finally shape the horde toward the image of God and hew from it something decent and holy, a pure creation, dedicated to the Invisible One—this is what his spirit and his wrists were craving.

The destination was the oasis of Kadesh. Just as the wilderness of Sur abutted the wilderness of Paran, so the latter abutted the wilderness of Sin on the south—but not everywhere and not directly. Somewhere in between lay the oasis of Kadesh, by contrast a delightful plain, a green breathing space in the arid land, with three robust springs and a number of smaller ones, too, a day's journey long and half a day's wide, dotted with fresh pastures and farmland, an alluring stretch of land rich in animals and vegetation and large enough to shelter and nourish a headcount like theirs.

Yehoshua knew about this attractive little piece of land, which was very clearly marked on the map he carried in his mind. Moses knew about it, too, but the fact that they chose Kadesh as their destination and headed off for it was Joshua's doing. Here was his opportunity. A pearl such as Kadesh, of course, did not just sit there without an owner, that goes without saying. It was in firm hands—but not too firm, Joshua was hoping. If they wanted to have it, they would have to fight for it against the man who controlled it, and that man was Amalek.

Some of the Amalekite clan had possession of Kadesh and would defend it. Joshua made it clear to Moses that there would have to be a war, a battle between Yahweh and Amalek, even if it should result in an eternal enmity between them, from generation to generation. They had to have the oasis; it was the perfect space for growth as well as for sanctification.

Moses was dubious. He believed that one of the implications of God's invisibility was that you shouldn't covet your neighbor's house, and he reproached his disciple to this effect. But the latter answered that Kadesh was not Amalek's house, and if he knew all about space he also knew all about times past, and he knew that previously (of course he couldn't say when) Kadesh had been inhabited by Hebrew people, blood kin, descendants of their fathers, who had been scattered by the Amalekites. Kadesh had been robbed from them, and what had been robbed could be robbed back.

Moses doubted that, but he had his own reasons for thinking that Kadesh was actually Yahweh's territory and should be accorded to those who were in covenant with Yahweh. It wasn't just because of its natural charms that Kadesh was named as it was, that is to say, "Sanctuary." In a certain sense it was the sanctuary of the Midianite

THOMAS MANN

Yahweh, whom Moses had recognized as the God of his fathers. Not far away, toward the east and toward Edom in a line of other mountains, lay Mount Horeb, which Moses had visited from Midian and on whose slope the God had revealed Himself to him in a burning bush. Horeb, the mountain, was Yahweh's seat—one of them, at least. His original seat, Moses knew, was Mount Sinai, in the mountain range that lay toward the deep midday. But between Sinai and Horeb, the site of Moses' commissioning, there was a close connection. After all, Yahweh sat upon both of them: you could equate them, you could call Horeb Sinai, too, and Kadesh was named as it was because, loosely speaking, it lay at the foot of the holy mount.

For that reason, Moses agreed to Joshua's plan and let him prepare for Yahweh's campaign against Amalek.

TWELVE

THE BATTLE took place—this is an historical fact—and it was a very difficult battle, seesawing back and forth. But Israel emerged triumphant. Moses actually conferred this name, Israel, which means "God wages war," on his blood kin before the battle, to give them strength, explaining that it was a very old name that had simply fallen into oblivion; even Jacob, the patriarch, had taken it and called his people by it. This served the blood kin well: however loosely their tribes had been connected, they were now all called Israel, and they fought united under this bellicose name, assembled in battle ranks and led by Joshua, the commanding young man, and Caleb, his lieutenant.

The Amalekites had had no doubts about what the approach of this mass of wandering people meant; approaches like that can mean only one thing. Without waiting for an attack on the oasis, they had come out into the desert in full force, larger than Israel in their numbers, and better armed, too, and amid high-swirling dust, turmoil, and battle cries, the struggle ensued. Joshua's people suffered an added disadvantage, being tormented by thirst and for many days having eaten only manna. But as recompense they had Joshua, the young man with the straight gaze, who directed their movements, and they had Moses, the man of God.

At the beginning of the skirmish, Moses withdrew along with Aaron, his half-brother, and Miriam, the prophetess, to a hill from which they could overlook the battlefield. His manliness was not of a warlike sort. Rather, it was his priestly function (and everyone agreed without hesitation that this alone could be his function) to lift up his arms and call upon God in incendiary phrases, for example, "Rise up, Yahweh, before the myriads, before Israel's thousands, so that Your enemies disperse, so that Your haters flee from Your visage!"

They did not flee and they did not disperse, or if they did, only nearby and quite temporarily; for although it is true that Israel was enraged by thirst and surfeit of manna, there were more of Amalek's myriads, and after a passing loss of nerve they kept advancing, at times dangerously close to the lookout hill. But it proved true without exception that as long as Moses kept his arms raised in prayer toward heaven, Israel prevailed, though if he let his arms sink down, then Amalek would triumph. For that reason, and because he could not keep his arms raised uninterruptedly on his own, both Aaron and Miriam supported him under his armpits and also grabbed onto his arms so that they would stay up. You can imagine what that entailed by reckoning that the battle lasted from morning until evening, in all of which time Moses had to maintain his painful posture. You see how hard it can be for spiritual manliness up on its prayer-hill— certainly harder than for the men who slug it out down below in the fray.

Nor could they keep it up the whole day long; now and then his companions had to lower the master's arms for a moment, but that always cost the Yahweh fighters much blood and distress. So his supporters hoisted his arms again, and the people down below gained new courage at the sight. They also profited from their commander Yehoshua's talent in leading the battle to a favorable conclusion. He was a strategic young warrior with ideas and objectives, who thought up maneuvers that were completely new, unheard of to that point in time, at least in the wilderness; and he was also a commander with nerves strong enough to tolerate a temporary abandonment of territory.

He gathered a selection of his best forces, the angels of death, at the right wing of his enemy, pressed toward it decisively, repelled it, and claimed victory at this position, although Amalek's main force meanwhile enjoyed a great advantage over Israel's ranks, storming ahead and winning a lot of territory from them. But by means of his breakthrough on their flank, Yehoshua reached Amalek's back, obliging him to turn toward him while at the same time fighting Israel's main forces, which had almost been defeated but were now advancing again with new energy. All this caused Amalek to lose his head and despair of his mission. "Treachery!" he cried. "All is lost! Hope no more for victory! Yahweh is above us, a god of fathomless perfidy!" And with this despairing formulation, Amalek let the sword sink from his hands and was cut down.

Only a few of his people were able to flee to the north, where they were reunited with their main clan. Israel, however, moved into the oasis of Kadesh, which proved to be traversed by a wide, rushing brook, lined with seed-bearing shrubs and fruit trees, and filled with bees, songbirds, quails, and hares. The children of Amalek who were left in the settlements increased the number of Israel's descendants. Amalek's women became wives and maidservants of Israel.

THIRTEEN

AₗₜₕₒᵤGₕ ₕᵢₛ ₐᵣₘₛ continued to pain him for a long time, Moses was a happy man. He also remained a much-burdened one, above all men on earth, as will be shown. But for now he was very happy about the way things were progressing. The emigration had been a success, Pharaoh's avenging forces had drowned in the Sea of Reeds, the journey in the wilderness had gone off smoothly, and with Yahweh's help the battle for Kadesh had ended in victory. He stood there before his father's blood kin, regal in the recognition of his success, as "the man Moses, who led us out of Egypt," and that was what he needed to begin the work he craved—the work of purifying and shaping in the name of the Invisible One, of drilling, chipping away, and forming flesh and blood. He was truly happy now to have this flesh set apart for him in open land, in the oasis called Sanctuary. It was his workshop.

He showed the people the mountain that was visible among the other mountains across the desert east of Kadesh: Horeb, which could also be called Sinai, thickly bestrewn with bushes two-thirds of the way up, and bare on top, Yahweh's seat. Such a designation seemed plausible, for it was a strange mountain, distinguished from its sisters by an unmoving cloud that lay above its peak like a roof. And while it appeared gray by day, at night it glowed. It was there, so the people heard, on the bushy slope of the mountain, below its rocky peak, that Yahweh had spoken to Moses out of the burning bush and had commissioned him to lead them out of Egypt. They heard about it with fear and trembling, for they were not yet capable of awe and reverence. In truth, all of them, even the graybeards, would always wobble at the knees like hysterical ninnies whenever Moses pointed out the mountain with the perpetual cloud and informed them that this was the home of a God who had taken a fancy to them and wanted to be their sole God. Shaking his fists, Moses scolded them about their crude behavior and gamely made it his concern to gird them for a closer relationship with Yahweh by establishing a shrine for Him right there in their midst, right in Kadesh.

For Yahweh had a roaming presence—this, like so much else, was related to His invisibility. He sat upon Sinai, He sat upon Horeb, and now, hardly had they ensconced themselves a little in the Amalekites' settlements, before Moses created a home for Him in Kadesh, in a tent near his own, which he called the meeting tent or gathering tent, and also the tabernacle, and where he housed holy objects as aids for worshiping the Imageless

One. They were primarily things that Moses remembered and borrowed from the cult of the Midianite Yahweh: a kind of chest, above all, with carrying poles, on which, according to Moses (and he had to know), the godhead was enthroned invisible and which you could take along out to the field and carry before you into battle, should Amalek, for example, try to close in on them and take revenge. An iron rod with a serpent's head, also dubbed the Iron Serpent, was stored next to the ark to commemorate Aaron's well-intended trick before Pharaoh, but also with the added symbolism of being the rod that Moses had extended over the Sea of Reeds to make it part. Especially, however, the Yahweh-tent sheltered the so-called ephod, the tossing-pouch from which sprang Urim and Thummim, the lots of the oracle—as a yes or no, a right or wrong, a good or evil—whenever a difficult, humanly unsolvable dispute forced them to appeal directly to Yahweh's arbitration.

In the disputes and legal questions that cropped up among the people, it was usually Moses himself who judged in Yahweh's place. In fact, the first thing he did in Kadesh was to establish a tribunal where he settled disputes on certain days and administered justice: there at the source of the most abundant spring, which had always been called Me-Meribah, that is to say, "Litigation Waters," there he administered justice and let it flow from him in holiness, the way the water sprang from the earth. Considering, however, that he alone had judicial authority over a total of twelve thousand five hundred souls, we can appreciate the burden he had to carry.

Since justice was something quite new to the abandoned and lost blood kin, who until now had hardly even known that it existed, all the more justice seekers came rushing continually to his spring site. There they learned, first, that justice was directly connected to and protected by the invisibility of God and His holiness; but second, that it also encompassed injustice, something it took the rabble a long time to comprehend, for they thought that anywhere that justice was flowing, everybody would have to have justice on their side. At first they didn't want to believe that someone could also receive justice by being judged in the wrong and having to slink off disappointed. Such a person might well regret that he hadn't settled his dispute by following earlier methods, by means of a stone in the fist, which might have led to a different outcome. Only with great effort did he learn from Moses that this would have challenged God's invisibility, and that no one whom justice had judged wrong should slink off disappointed; for in its holy invisibility, justice was both beautiful and dignified, whether it judged you right or wrong.

So Moses had not only to administer justice, but also to teach justice, and was much burdened. In his Theban boarding school, he himself had studied law, Egyptian legal scrolls and the codex of Hammurabi, the king by the

Euphrates. That knowledge helped him clarify his judgments in many of the cases that came before him, as for example: If an ox had gored a man or a woman to death, the ox was to be stoned and its flesh was not to be eaten, but the owner of the ox was innocent, unless the ox was wont to push with its horns and the owner had not kept it in; in that case, the owner's life was forfeit, too, unless he could redeem it with thirty silver shekels. Or if someone dug an open pit without covering it over properly, so that an ox or an ass fell in, then the owner of the pit should recompense the loss with money, although the carcass should belong to him; and other such instances of bodily harm, maltreatment of slaves, theft and burglary, crop damage, arson, and breach of trust. In all these cases and a hundred more, Moses, imitating Hammurabi, made judgments, determined right and wrong. But there were too many cases for one judge, and the spring site was overflowing. If the master investigated an individual incident at all responsibly, there was no end to it. He often had to defer, new cases were always accumulating, and he was burdened above all men.

FOURTEEN

For that reason it was a great stroke of luck that his brother-in-law Jethro from Midian paid him a visit in Kadesh and offered him a piece of good advice, which given his conscientious self-reliance, he would not have discovered on his own. Soon after his arrival in the oasis, Moses had requested that his brother-by-marriage send back to him his wife, Zipporah, and his two sons, who had been sheltered in Jethro's tent down in Midian during the Egyptian tribulations. And Jethro was good enough to come himself, to hand over wife and sons personally, to embrace Moses, take a look around, and hear from him how everything had gone.

He was a portly, cheerful sheik, with graceful, deft gestures, a man of the world, prince of a civilized, socially sophisticated people. Welcomed with great ceremony, he took up lodging with Moses in his tent, and heard not without amazement how one of his own gods, indeed the invisible one (wouldn't you know it), had done so extremely well for Moses and his people and how he had managed to rescue them from the hand of the Egyptians.

"Who would have thought!" he said. "Apparently he's greater than we supposed, and what you're telling me makes me inclined to worry that we've been remiss in our attentions thus far. I'll make sure that we, too, accord him greater honor in the future."

For the following day, Moses scheduled public burnt offerings, something he rarely did. He didn't think especially much of offerings; they weren't vital, he said, before the Invisible One—and others, the people of the world, were in the habit of performing them. Yahweh had said, "Obey my voice above all else, that is: the voice of my servant Moses, and then I shall be your God and you My people." But on this occasion, there were butchered and burnt offerings, both for Yahweh's savoring and to celebrate Jethro's arrival. The following day, early in the morning, Moses took his brother-by-marriage along to the Litigation Waters so that he could attend court for a day and see how Moses sat in judgment over his people, who stood around him from morning until evening. There was no hope of getting through it all.

"Now I beg you for heaven's sake, my dear brother-in-law," said the guest as he left the tribunal with Moses, "look at how you're burdening yourself! Sitting there alone, and everyone and his brother standing around you from morning until evening! Why are you doing that?"

"I have to," answered Moses. "The people come to me so that I'll judge between each one and his neighbor and show them God's justice and His laws."

"But my dear fellow, how can anyone be so hapless!" said Jethro in reply. "Is that the way to govern? Does a ruler have to drive himself so hard by doing everything on his own? You're exhausting yourself so, it's a terrible shame. You can hardly see out of your eyes, and you've lost your voice from judging. And the people are no less tired. This is not the way to go about it; you can't go on forever settling every matter yourself. It isn't even necessary—listen to me! If you represent the people before God and bring the important matters, the ones that concern everybody, before Him, that's quite enough. But," he said gesturing easily, "go find law-abiding, more or less respected people among your horde, and set them above the others: above a thousand, above a hundred, even above fifty or ten, so that they can judge them according to the justice and according to the laws that you have presented to the people. Let them bring only the really important matters to you; the lesser ones they'll take care of themselves—you don't even have to know about them. I wouldn't have my little paunch and couldn't have gotten away to pay you a visit if I thought I had to know about everything and run in circles like you."

"But the judges will take gifts and will find for the godless ones," Moses answered dejectedly. "For gifts make seeing men blind and pervert the just man's cause."

"I know, I know," replied Jethro. "I'm quite aware of that. But that's the price you have to pay. If you're going to administer justice and create order, it doesn't matter so much if gifts complicate the situation a bit. Look, the ones who take gifts, they're ordinary folk, but the people are also composed of ordinary folk; that's why they appreciate what's ordinary and can adjust to it comfortably. Besides, if someone has his case subverted by a judge-over-ten, because the fellow took something from a godless one, then he should go through official channels and have recourse to legal process; he should call upon the judge-over-fifty and the judge-over-a-hundred and ultimately the judge-over-a-thousand, who gets more gifts than anyone and therefore has a clearer view. Your man will find justice with him, if he hasn't grown too bored with the whole thing by then."

Thus Jethro uttered his opinion with the graceful gestures that made life easier for all who saw them, showing that he was the priest-king of a civilized desert people. Moses listened to him dejectedly and nodded. He had the impressionable soul of a lonely, spiritual man who nods reflectively at the cleverness of the world and understands that it may well be correct. Indeed, he followed the advice of his deft brother-by-marriage—it was quite unavoidable. He appointed lay judges who let justice flow according to his teachings alongside the large spring and alongside the smaller ones. They adjudicated the run-of-the-mill cases (if an ass had fallen into a pit, for example), and only the capital cases came to him, God's priest, although the really big ones were decided by holy lots.

And so he was no longer excessively caught up in these matters, and instead had his arms freed for the further sculpting that he intended to do on the formless body of the people, and for which Joshua, the strategic young man, had won him a workshop, namely, the oasis of Kadesh. Justice was an important example of the implications of God's invisibility, certainly, but it was really only an example, and it would be a daunting, lengthy task, to be achieved with anger and with patience, this sculpting from the unruly horde not merely a people like other peoples—for whom the ordinary was comfortable—but rather an extraordinary people, a people apart, a pure creation, erected to the Invisible One and sanctified to Him.

FIFTEEN

THE BLOOD KIN soon realized what it meant to have fallen into the hands of a workman like Moses, both angry and patient, in service to the Invisible One. They realized that the unnatural directive to raise no cry of joy at their enemy's drowning had been only a beginning—it was in fact an anticipation, located far into the realm of purity and holiness, with many preconditions to be met before one could reach the point of experiencing a demand like that as not completely unnatural. The true nature of the horde and how much they were only raw material of flesh and blood, lacking the fundamentals of purity and holiness; how much Moses had to begin from the beginning and instruct them in first things—this can be seen by the primitive precepts with which he began to get to work on them, to chisel and to chip away—and not to their pleasure. The block of stone does not cheer for the master but against him, and the first things that happen during its formation seem to it the most unnatural of all.

Moses, with his wide-set eyes and his pushed-in nose, was always among them, now here, now there, now deep in one encampment and now in another, shaking his fists from their broad wrists. Carping and caviling, he joggled and straightened out their nature, reprimanded, aligned, and cleaned it up as needed, all the while taking as his touchstone the invisibility of God, of Yahweh, who had led them out of Egypt to take them as His people, and who wanted them to be a holy people, holy like Himself. At present they were nothing but rabble, which was demonstrated when they emptied their bodies wherever they happened to be, even in their camp. That was a disgrace and an affliction. You should have a place outside the camp to walk out to if it's needed, do you hear me? And you should have a little shovel to dig with before you sit down; and after you've sat down you should cover it over, for the Lord your God walks within your camp, which should therefore be a holy camp, namely, a clean one, so that He will not hold His nose and turn away from you. For holiness begins with cleanliness, and such purity in coarse things is the coarse beginning of all purity. Did you get that, Ahiman, and you, mistress Naemi? Next time I come by, I want to see everyone with a little shovel, or the angel of death shall be visited upon you!

You should be clean and bathe often with fresh water for the sake of your health, because without that, there can be no purity or holiness, and disease is unclean. If you think that vulgarity is healthier than clean practices, you are a fool and should be struck with jaundice, pimply warts, and the botch of Egypt. If you do not practice cleanliness, nasty black smallpox will erupt and the seeds of pestilence will spread from blood to blood. Learn to distinguish between purity and impurity; otherwise you will not endure before the Invisible One and will be only rabble. For that reason, if a man or woman has a canker-ous leprosy and an evil discharge on the body, or scabs or itches, that person is impure and will not be toler-ated within the camp, but must be put outside in front of it, set apart in impurity, just as the Lord has set you all apart, so that you can be pure. And whatever such a one has touched, or wherever he has lain, and the saddle on which he has ridden, that should be burned. But if he has become pure in his apartness, then he should count seven days to see if he is truly pure and bathe thoroughly with water, and then he can return again.

Distinguish! I say to you, and be holy before God. Otherwise you cannot be holy in the way I wish you to be. You eat everything all jumbled up, without discrim-ination or delicacy, as I've had to witness. I find that an abomination. Rather, you should eat certain things and not others, and hold to your pride and your disgust. Whatever animal has cloven hooves and chews the cud, that may you eat. But whatever chews the cud and has hooves that are not cloven, like the camel, that is unclean, and you should not eat it. Please note: the trusty camel is not impure as a living creature of God, but it is not suited as food, no more than is the pig, which you should not eat either, for it has cloven hooves, but does not chew the cud. And therefore distinguish!

Everything in the water that has fins and scales, that may you eat, but whatever is sliding around without them, salamanders and their ilk, they are also of God, to be sure, but as food they should be an aversion to you. Among the birds, you should spurn the eagle, the ossifrage, the osprey, the vulture, and their like; in addition all ravens, the ostrich, the nighthawk, the cuckoo, the screech owl, the swan, the great owl, the bat, the cormorant, the stork, the heron, and lapwing as well as the swallow. I forgot the hoopoe—you should avoid it, too. And who would want to eat a weasel, a mouse, a toad, or a hedgehog? Who is so rabble-like as to consume the lizard, the mole, and the slow-worm or anything else that creeps on the earth and crawls on its belly? But this you are doing and turning your souls into a cesspool! The next person I see eating a slow-worm will learn from me the hard way never to do it again. For even though he won't die from it and it will do him no harm, it is disgraceful, and there are many things that you should find disgraceful. And therefore you should eat no carrion. Besides, it's harmful.

And so he gave them precepts for eating and restricted them in matters of nourishment, but not only in these. He also did it in matters of lust and love, because in that realm, too, everything was topsy-turvy, in the way of true rabble. You should not break the marriage vow, he told them, for it is a holy barrier. But do you know what else is implied by not breaking the vow? It means a hundred restrictions for the sake of God's holiness, and not only that you should not covet your neighbor's wife—that is the least of it. For you live in the flesh, but are sworn to the Invisible One, and marriage is the epitome of all purity in the sight of God. For that reason you should not take a woman and her mother as well, to give only one example. That is unseemly. Nor should you ever, ever lie with your sister, to see her shame and she yours, for that is incest. You shouldn't even lie with your aunt, that is neither worthy of her nor of you, and you should shrink back from it. When a woman has her ailment, you should avoid her and not approach the source of her blood. And if something shameful happens to a man in his sleep, he shall be impure until the next evening and bathe himself assiduously in water.

I hear that you are urging your daughter into whoring and taking a whore's wages from her? Do that no more, for if you persist in it, I will have you stoned. What are you thinking of, to sleep with a boy as with a woman? That is an absurdity and an abomination among the people, and both of you should die for it. And if someone, be it a man or a woman, takes up with a beast, that person should be completely eradicated, and strangled along with the beast.

Just imagine their dismay at all these restrictions! At first they had the feeling that if they adhered to all these things life as they knew it would be no more. He was chipping away at them with the chisel so that the chips were flying, and that was to be taken very literally, for he wasn't joking about the punishments to be meted out for the worst transgressions, and backing up his interdictions stood young Joshua and his angels of death.

"I am the Lord thy God," Moses said, running the risk that they might in truth take him for God, "who brought you out of the land of Egypt and set you apart from all peoples. For that reason, you too should set apart the pure from the impure and not follow other peoples in whoredom, but be holy unto Me. For I, the Lord, am holy and have set you apart so you can be Mine. The most impure thing of all is to attend to any god but Me, for I am a jealous God. The most impure thing of all is to make an image, whether it look like a man or a woman, an ox or a hawk, a fish or a worm, for if you do that it is apostasy against Me, even if the image is meant to represent Me, and you might just as well sleep with your sister or with a beast—it's but a small step from one to the other.

"Be on guard! I am among you and see everything. If anyone goes whoring with the Egyptian gods of animals or the dead, I will seek vengeance. I will chase him into the desert and cut him off like an outcast. If anyone makes sacrifices to Moloch (who still lives in your memory, as I know well), expending his strength for him, he is a bad person and I will treat him badly. And for that reason you should not allow your son or your daughter to follow the foolish custom of walking through fire, nor pay heed to the flight and cry of birds, nor whisper with diviners, observers of times, and enchanters, nor should you consult with the dead or do magic with My name. If anyone is a scoundrel and invokes My name in witness, he does so with utmost futility, and I will consume him. But even to tattoo yourself, to shave the hair of your eyebrows, and to cut your face in mourning is magic and an abomination among the people—I will not tolerate it."

How great was their consternation! They weren't even to cut themselves in mourning or get a few tattoos. So that's what having an invisible God entailed! Being in a covenant with Yahweh meant big restrictions. But since the angel of death stood behind what Moses was forbidding and since they didn't especially want to be chased into the desert, the forbidden things soon came to seem dreadful to them—at first only in connection with the punishment; but that punishment soon led to their branding the deed as bad, and at its commission they felt bad themselves, without even thinking about punishment.

Rein in your heart, he said to them, and do not cast your eye on another person's possessions, thinking how you would like to have them, for that will easily lead you to take them from him, whether by furtive stealing, which is cowardly, or by murder, which is brutal. Yahweh and I want you to be neither cowardly nor brutal, but rather you should be in the middle, that is to say, decent. Have you understood that much? Stealing is a creeping misery, but to murder, whether from rage or greed or greedy rage or raging greed, that is a blazing atrocity, and whoever commits it, I will set my face against him so that he will not know where to hide. For he has spilled blood, where blood is a holy aversion and a great mystery, a gift upon My altar and an atonement. You should eat no blood and no flesh that has been in blood, for blood is Mine. But whoever might be smeared with the blood of a human, his heart should sicken in cold horror, and I will hunt him so that he will run away from his own self to the ends of the earth. And all say Amen!

And they said Amen, still hoping that by murder He meant only killing, which not many of them were interested in, or at least only occasionally. But it turned out that Yahweh interpreted the word as broadly as He did adultery, and understood all sorts of things by it, so that murder and killing were defined very loosely. With every injury of another person through deceit or fraud, to which nearly all of them were inclined, blood was spilled. They were not to deal deceitfully with one another, nor make statements as false witnesses; they should use just measures, just pounds and just bushels. It was highly unnatural, and for now it was only the natural fear of punishment that cast an air of naturalness on commandment and taboo.

That you should honor your father and your mother, as Moses demanded, likewise had a wider meaning than was suspected at the outset. Whoever raised his hand against his progenitors and cursed them—well, all right, he would take them to task. But the honoring was to extend even to those who only *might* have been your progenitors. In front of any hoary head, you should rise, cross your arms, and bow your silly head, do you understand me? That's what decency in God's eyes requires. (The only comfort was that since your neighbor wasn't allowed to kill anyone, you had good prospects of becoming old and hoary yourself, so that others would then have to rise in front of you.)

In the end, however, it appeared that old age was a symbol for old things in general, for everything that was not of today or yesterday, but that came from a great distance—pious traditions, ancestral customs. They were to be honored and revered. Thus you should sanctify My holidays: the day I brought you out of Egypt, the day of unleavened bread, and always, the day I rested from the work of creation. You should not defile My day, the Sabbath, by the sweat of toil, I forbid you to do that! For with a mighty hand and an extended arm I have brought you out of the Egyptian house of bondage, where you were a servant and a beast of burden, and My day should be the day of your freedom, and you should keep it holy. For six days you should be a farmer or a plow-maker or a potter or a coppersmith or a carpenter, but on My day you should put on clean garments and be nothing other than a human being and lift up your eyes to the Invisible One.

You were abused servants in the land of Egypt— remember that in your conduct toward those who are strangers among you, Amalek's children, for example, whom God gave into your hands. Do not abuse them! Esteem them as you would yourself and give them equal justice, or else I, Myself, will intervene, for they stand under Yahweh's protection. In general, when distinguishing between yourself and others, don't be so foolish as to think you are the only one who is real or who counts, and that the other person is just an illusion. Life is common to both of you, and it is only chance that you are not he. For that reason, do not love yourself alone, but love him likewise, and treat him as you would wish him to treat you if he were you! Be cordial with one another and kiss your fingertips when you walk by one another and bow courteously and speak the greeting, "Be well and healthy!" For it is just as important that he is healthy as that you are. And even if it is only outward courtesy to do this and kiss your fingertips, nevertheless the gesture will instill in your heart something of what you should feel toward your neighbor.—Say Amen to all of that!

And they said Amen.

SIXTEEN

B<small>UT THE</small> A<small>MEN</small> did not count for much. They said it
only because he was the man who'd had the good for-
tune to lead them out of Egypt, sink Pharaoh's chariots,
and win the battle for Kadesh. It took them a long time
to absorb more or less, or maybe only apparently, what
he taught and imposed upon them—the restrictions,
the commandments and taboos. It was a daunting piece
of work that he was taking upon himself, to erect from
out of the horde a holy people for the Lord, a pure creation, which would be worthy to stand before the Invisible One. By the sweat of his brow, he worked away at it
in Kadesh, his workshop, keeping his wide-set eyes everywhere—he carved, chipped, shaped, and smoothed the
unwilling block of stone with a dogged patience, with
repeated forbearance and frequent indulgence, with blazing anger and punitive implacability.

He often wanted to give up when the flesh on which
he was working proved to be intractable, forgetful, prone
to relapse, when the people failed to dig with their little
shovels or ate slow-worms or slept with their sisters or

even with beasts, tattooed themselves, whispered with diviners, crept into thievery, and killed one another. "O you rabble!" he would then say to them. "You'll see. The Lord will suddenly descend upon you and destroy you." But to the Lord Himself he would say, "What am I supposed to do with this flesh, and why have You withdrawn Your mercy from me, to saddle me with something I cannot carry? I would rather muck out a stall that has gone seven years without spade or water, or clear a jungle into an orchard with my bare hands, than try to fashion a pure form for You from these people. How did I come to be the one to carry them in my arms as if I had given birth to them? I'm only half-related to them, on my father's side. And for that reason, I beg You, let me enjoy my life, and release me from this task or strangle me instead!"

But God answered him from within his heart with such a clear voice that he heard it with his ears and fell prostrate upon the ground:

"Precisely because you are only half-related to them, on your hastily buried father's side, you are just the man to work on them for Me and to raise them up before Me into a holy people. For if you were right there with them and were truly one of them, you would not be able to see them as they are nor put your hand to them. Besides, when you wail at Me and try to get out of your work, that's all just affectation, for you realize that it's already starting to take hold, that you've already given them a conscience, and that they feel bad when they do bad things. So don't pretend that you don't greatly fancy your burden. It is My own fancy that you share, God's fancy, and without it, life would be revolting to you, as manna was to the people after just a few days. Only if I were to strangle you, in fact, could you really do without them."

The burdened man understood that, nodded his head at Yahweh's words as he lay face-down, and then stood up to assume his burden again. But it was not simply as a sculptor of the people that he was a burdened man—the burden and the grief reached right into his family life. There was aggravation, envy, and strife on his account, and no peace in his tent. And he was to blame, if you like, for his senses were the cause of his troubles—they had been aroused by his work and were in thrall to an African woman, the famous Ethiopian.

We know that in addition to his first wife, Zipporah, the mother of his sons, he was living at the time with an Ethiopian—a woman from the land of Kush who had arrived in Egypt as a child, lived among the blood kin in Goshen, and joined the exodus. There was no doubt that she had known many men, but Moses nevertheless took her to himself to share his bed. She was a splendid specimen in her way, with mountainous breasts, rolling eye-whites, full lips (to sink into them in a kiss must have been a great adventure), and skin fragrant with spices. Moses was utterly devoted to her for his recreational pleasure and could not keep away from her even though it meant bearing the enmity of his whole household, not only of his Midianite wife and their sons, but especially of his half-siblings, Miriam and Aaron.

Zipporah, who had much of the graceful worldliness of her brother Jethro, was able to put up with her rival tolerably well, especially because the woman kept her female triumph quiet, behaving with great deference in Zipporah's presence. She treated the Ethiopian more with mockery than with hatred and also confronted Moses about the affair with some irony, rather than giving full rein to her jealousy. And their sons, Gershom and Eliezer, who were members of Joshua's armed band, were too highly disciplined to rebel against their father; one could tell only that they were irritated and ashamed because of him.

Things were quite different with Miriam, the prophetess, and the unctuous Aaron. Their hatred of the Ethiopian bedmate was more venomous than the others' because it was more or less an outlet for a deeper and broader resentment that united them against Moses. For a long time now, they had begun to envy him his close relationship to God, his spiritual mastery, his having been chosen for the work, which they thought was mostly conceit. They believed that they were just as good as he, in fact better, and said to one another, "Does the Lord speak only through Moses? Doesn't He also speak through us?

Who is this man Moses to have raised himself above us like this?" This was the underlying reason for their taking offense at his relationship with the Ethiopian woman, and whenever they pressed their brother, to his sorrow, nagging him about his nights of passion, their reproaches were only the starting point for further accusations. They soon moved on to the injustice inflicted on them by his elevation.

Once, then, as the sun was setting, they were in his tent with him and harrying him, as I've said, in their habitual manner: the Ethiopian woman this and the Ethiopian woman that, and how he was devoted to her black breasts and what a scandal it was, what a disgrace for Zipporah, his first wife, and how compromising for Moses himself who was claiming to be a prince of God and Yahweh's sole earthly spokesman . . .

"Claiming?" he said. "What God has commanded me to be, that is what I am. But how hateful of you, how really and truly hateful, to begrudge me my pleasure and recreation at my Ethiopian's breasts! For it is no sin before God, and among all the interdictions that he gave me there is none that says one should not lie with an Ethiopian woman. Nothing that I'm aware of."

Look at that, they said. He's trying to handpick the interdictions that suit him. The next thing you know he'll suggest that we're actually commanded to lie with Ethiopian women, because he thinks he is Yahweh's sole spokesman. But all the while they, Miriam and Aaron, were the true children of Amram, grandson of Levi, whereas when all was said and done, he was only a foundling from the reeds and should learn a little humility, for by demanding to keep his Ethiopian, whatever the aggravation, he was only revealing his pride and arrogance.

"Can I help it if I have been appointed?" he said. "Can I help it if I stumble upon a burning bush? Miriam, I've always esteemed your prophetic gifts and never denied how good you are on the timbrel . . ."

"Then why did you forbid me to sing my hymn 'Horse and Rider,'" she asked, "and keep me from drumming to the women's dance, just because God allegedly forbade His armies to rejoice at the Egyptians' demise? That was horrid of you!"

"And you, Aaron," the assailed man continued, "I took you on as high priest in the tabernacle and delegated to you the ark, the ephod, and the Iron Serpent, so that you would attend to them. That's how much I esteem you."

"That was the least you could do," replied Aaron, "for your own tongue is so awkward that you would never have won the people over to Yahweh without my eloquence or stirred them to an exodus. Yet you call yourself the man who led us out of Egypt. But if you really esteem us and aren't lording it arrogantly over your rightful siblings, why won't you listen to what we're saying and why do you remain deaf when we warn you that you're bringing danger upon our whole clan with your dark lust? For it is a cup of bitter gall for Zipporah, your Midianite wife, and by it you're affronting all of Midian, so that Jethro, your brother-by-marriage, will end up by bringing war upon us, and all for the sake of your black dalliance."

"Jethro," said Moses with great self-control, "is a graceful, civilized gentleman who will understand quite well that Zipporah—may her name be praised!—no longer has anything to offer for the requisite recreation of a severely burdened and overworked man like me. The skin of my Ethiopian, however, is like cinnamon and carnation oil in my nose. I am devoted to her with all my being, and for that reason I implore you, dear friends, grant her to me, please!"

But they didn't want to do that. Squawking, they demanded not only that he separate from the Ethiopian woman and banish her from his bed, but also that he cast her out into the desert without water.

At that, the vein in Moses' forehead throbbed in anger and his fists began to tremble violently by his thighs. But before he could open his mouth to utter a rejoinder, there occurred a quite different trembling—Yahweh stepped in, set His face against the hard-hearted siblings, and took the part of His servant Moses in a way they would never forget. There occurred something terrible and utterly unprecedented.

SEVENTEEN

THE FOUNDATIONS trembled. The earth jolted and vi-
brated and lurched under their feet so that they could
not stay upright, and all three staggered back and forth in
the tent, whose support poles were shaken as if by gigan-
tic fists. The structure did not reel in one direction only,
however, but to all sides at once in a terrifyingly intricate
and dizzying motion, while at the same time was heard
a subterranean roaring and rumbling and, from above
and without, a blast as from a blaring trumpet, along
with more booming, thundering, and crackling. It is very
strange and singularly embarrassing if you are just about
to erupt in anger when the Lord takes the words out of
your mouth and erupts Himself—much more powerfully
than you could have done—shaking the world, while you
could only have shaken your fists.

Of the three, Moses was least pale with fear, for he
was always braced for God. But together with Aaron
and Miriam, who were fearfully pale indeed, he rushed
out of the house. They saw that the earth had opened its
maw and that a great crevice was gaping right in front of

the tent. It had obviously been intended for Miriam and Aaron, and if it hadn't missed them by only a couple of ells, the earth would have swallowed them both. And they saw the mountain in the morning beyond the desert, Horeb or Sinai—yes, they saw what was happening with Horeb and what was going on with Mount Sinai! It stood completely covered by smoke and flames, hurling glowing rocks toward the sky with a distant cracking roar as streams of fire ran down its sides. Its lightning-laced smoldering darkened the stars above the desert, and over the oasis of Kadesh a slow rain of ashes began to fall.

Aaron and Miriam prostrated themselves, for they were terrified by the crevice meant for them, and from the revelation of Yahweh on the mountain they understood that they had gone too far and spoken foolishly. Aaron called out:

"Oh, my master, this woman, my sister, has babbled hatefully. Please accept my plea and do not allow the sin of sinning against the Lord's anointed to stay upon her!"

And Miriam also cried out to Moses and spoke:

"Master, no one could speak more foolishly than did my brother Aaron. Forgive him, please, and remove the sin from him so that God will not swallow him up for having teased you so irresponsibly about your Ethiopian woman!"

Moses was not quite sure whether Yahweh's manifestation was really intended for his siblings and their lack of feeling or whether it was only by coincidence that He had summoned him just then to talk about the people and the work of forming them—for at every hour, Moses expected that kind of call. But he left Aaron and Miriam to assume what they would, and answered:

"There you have it. But take heart, children of Amram, I will put in a good word for you with God up there on the mountain where He calls me. For now you shall see, and all the people shall see, whether your brother has been weakened by his black courtship or whether a godlike courage resides in his heart as in no one else's. Up to the fiery mountain I shall go, quite alone, to God on high, to hear His thoughts and fearlessly engage the Fearful One in a frank and open conversation, far from mankind, but on their behalf. For I've long known that He wants to make everything I've taught them about their sanctification before Him, the Holy One, into something compact, both pithy and everlasting, so that I can carry it down to you from His mountain and so that the people can possess it in the tabernacle, along with the ark, the ephod, and the Iron Serpent. Farewell! I may perish in God's turbulence and in the fires of the mountain—that may well be, and I must reckon with that. But if I return, I will bring down for you out of His thunder the pithy, everlasting code, God's law."

This really was his firm intention; he had decided on it as a matter of life and death. For in order to root the horde, the stiff-necked, relapsing horde, in God's morality and make them fear the commandments, there was nothing more effective than to dare to ascend utterly alone into Yahweh's terror high on the spewing mountain, and from there to carry down the dictates. Then, he thought, they'll stick to them. And for that reason, as they came running to his tent from every direction, their knees knocking at these omens and at the rupturing roll of the earth—which was repeated once and then twice more weakly—he rebuked them for their vulgar quivering and encouraged them to pull themselves together. God was calling him on their behalf, he said, and he intended to ascend to Yahweh on the mountaintop and bring a little something back for them, God willing. They, however, were to go home and together prepare for a journey. They were to sanctify themselves and wash their clothes and refrain from their women, for on the morrow they were to move out of Kadesh into the wilderness, closer to the mountain, and opposite it they were to set up a camp and wait for him there until he returned from the terrible rendezvous, bringing a little something back for them, perhaps.

And thus it happened, more or less. For Moses, as was his way, had thought to tell them only that they should wash their clothes and keep away from their women, but Joshua ben Nun, the strategic young man, was mindful of what else was necessary for this kind of expedition. With his troops, he arranged for everything that thousands in the wilderness would require in the way of water and nourishment; he even arranged for a courier service between Kadesh and the outer camp opposite the mountain. He left Caleb, his lieutenant, and a police division behind in Kadesh with those who were not able or did not want to come along. And when the third day had arrived and all the preparations had been made, the others moved out toward the mountain with their carts and cattle, a journey of one and a half days. Joshua made them a compound there, still at a reasonable distance from Yahweh's smoldering seat, and in Moses' name strictly forbade them to so much as think about ascending the mountain themselves or even touching its foot: To approach so near to God was reserved for the master alone; you'd be risking your life, and whoever laid hand on the mountain should be stoned or shot with bow and arrow. They had no trouble accepting that, for rabble have no desire to get too close to God; and to the ordinary man, the mountain did not look in the least inviting, not by day, when Yahweh stood upon it in a thick cloud shot through with lightning, and certainly not by night, when the cloud and the entire peak were aglow.

Joshua was extraordinarily proud of the godlike courage of his leader who, already on the first day, in front of everyone, had set out alone and on foot, his walking-staff in hand, equipped only with an earthenware flask, a couple of rolls, and some tools (pickaxe, chisel, scraper, and graver), on the road to the mountain. The young man was very proud of him and happy about the impression that this kind of holy audacity must make upon the multitudes. But he was worried about the revered man, too, and had entreated him not to risk coming too close to Yahweh and to watch out for the molten ooze that was running down the sides of the mountain. Apart from that, he had said, he would visit him up there now and then, to make sure that everything was provided for, so the master would not lack the basic necessities in God's wilderness.

EIGHTEEN

So Moses crossed the desert, his staff at his side, his wide-set eyes focused on God's mountain, which was smoking like an oven and spewing frequently. The mountain was shaped peculiarly, riddled with fissures and ridges that seemed to divide it into different levels and resembled ascending paths, but were in actuality only gradations of yellow walls. On the third day, the appointed one passed beyond the mountain's foothills and arrived at its craggy base. There he began to climb up, his fist closed around the walking-staff that tested his way, climbing ramble-scramble through blackened, scalded shrubs, hour after hour, step by step, ever higher into God's vicinity, as far as it was possible for a human being to go, for eventually the sulfurous fumes that pervaded the air, redolent of hot metals, robbed him of breath, and he was seized with coughing. Nevertheless, he reached the uppermost ridge and terrace underneath the peak, where there was a wide view of the bare, rugged mountain chain on either side and beyond, into the desert stretching out before him right up to Kadesh. Nearer to him, his people's compound was visible, too, tiny in the depths below.

Here, in a mountain wall, the coughing Moses found a cave with a rocky overhang that could protect him from falling stones and flowing ooze. He took up residence there and made himself at home so that, after briefly stopping to catch his breath, he could tackle the work that God had ordered him to do and that would keep him busy under arduous conditions (for the metallic fumes still weighed on his chest and even made the water taste like sulfur) for no less than forty days and forty nights.

But why would it take so long? Silly question! The pithy, everlasting code, the compact contract, God's condensed moral law, was to be secured and graved into the stone of His mountain so that Moses could carry it down to the wavering rabble, the blood of his hastily buried father, into the compound where they were waiting. There it was to stand among them inviolable, from generation to generation, engraved in their hearts and in their flesh and blood, as well: the quintessence of human decency. From within Moses' breast, God loudly ordered him to carve two tablets out of the mountain and to write His dictates there, five phrases on one of them and five on the other, ten phrases all told. It was no small matter to shape the tablets, to smooth them down and make them reasonably worthy bearers of the pithy, everlasting code. For a solitary man (even if he did have broad wrists and had drunk the milk of a stone-carver's daughter), it was a piece of work susceptible to many setbacks and would claim all of one-fourth of his forty days. But the inscribing was a problem whose solution could easily have increased the number of Moses' days on the mountain to even more than forty.

For how was he to write? In his Theban boarding school, he had acquired both the decorative pictorial language of Egypt together with its everyday forms, as well as the wondrous, wedged crush of triangles from the Euphrates, in which the kings of the world exchanged their thoughts on clay fragments. Besides that, he had made the acquaintance among the Midianites of a third hieroglyphic magic, commonly used in Sinai and composed of eyes, crosses, beetles, semi-circles, and variously-shaped serpentine lines, which had been copied from the pictures of Egypt with the clumsiness of the desert. Those marks, however, did not indicate whole words, objects, or ideas, but rather only portions of them, open syllables that were supposed to be read together. None of these three methods of pinning down thought appealed to him—for the simple reason that each of them was tied to the spoken language that it represented, and it was perfectly clear to Moses that he could never under any circumstances commit the ten-phrase dictation to stone in Babylonian, Egyptian, or in the Bedouin patois of Sinai.

Only in the language of his father's blood kin could that happen, should that happen—in the dialect that they spoke and that he employed to work on them and their morals—whether or not they'd be able to read it. And how were they going to read it, since no one had ever written it, and no hieroglyphic magic was available to represent their speech?

Moses fervently wished for something like that—that is, for something that they would quickly, very quickly, be able to read, something that children like them could learn in a few days, and thus something that he would have to devise and invent in a few days, God's help being so near. For devised and invented the lettering would have to be, since it didn't yet exist.

What a rushed and crushing assignment! He hadn't considered it in advance at all; he had simply thought "write," and not borne in mind that you can't just write without further ado, just like that. It made his head glow and smoke like an oven and like the mountain peak, ablaze with his fervently populist wish. It seemed to him as if rays were emanating from his head, as if horns were growing out of his forehead from the strain of wishing and from one clear insight. He wouldn't be able to invent signs for all the words that his blood kin employed or for the syllables that composed their words. Even if the people down in the compound had a limited vocabulary, there would be too many marks to create in his limited number of days on the mountain, especially if they were supposed to be able to learn to read them rapidly. For that reason, he did it a different way, and horns rose out of his forehead from pride over his divine inspiration. He gathered together the sounds of the language that are formed by the lips, the tongue, and palate, and by the throat, while setting aside the few open sounds that appeared in the words intermittently, enclosed by the other sounds and becoming words only because of them. Nor were there excessively many of the articulated noises that preceded and followed them, hardly twenty; and if you lent them signs that called for agreement on how to hiss and huff, to mumble and rumble, to spit and smack, then, while leaving out the basic sounds that would result from them on their own, you could join the signs together into words and symbols—for any one of them, for all that existed, not only in the language of his father's blood kin, but in all languages. You could even write Egyptian with it, and Babylonian.

A divine inspiration! An idea with horns. It was just like Him from whom it came, the Invisible and Spiritual One, to whom the world belonged and who, although He had especially selected out the blood kin down below, was the Lord of the whole earth. It was also highly suited to its most immediate and urgent purpose, for which and from which it was born: the text of the tablets, the compact contract. To be sure, that text had been crafted first of all for the blood kin whom Moses had led out of Egypt, since both he and God had taken a fancy to them; but as this handful of signs could be used if need be to write the words of every language of every people, and since Yahweh was the God of the whole world, then the pithy code that Moses intended to write down was the sort that could serve as a basic directive and a rock of human decency among all the peoples of the earth—across the whole world.

So with his head afire, Moses, borrowing loosely from the people of the Sinai and using his graver, tried out on the rocky wall the signs for the babbling, banging, and bursting, the popping and hopping, slurring and purring sounds, and when he had artfully assembled the distinctive signs together—lo and behold, you could write the whole world with them, whatever occupied a space and whatever occupied no space, what was made and what was made-up—absolutely everything.

And so he wrote, which is to say, he engraved, chiseled, and scraped in the splintery stone of the tablets, having first made them with great effort, a task that had gone hand in hand with the creation of the letters. All of this lasted forty days—and no one should be surprised at that.

Joshua, his young man, came up to visit him a few times, to bring him water and flatbread, without the people needing, necessarily, to know of it; for they thought that Moses was being nourished up there solely by his nearness to God and his conversation, and for strategic reasons Joshua wanted this assumption to stand. That is why his visits were kept short and took place at night.

Moses, meanwhile, sat from the daylight's rising over Edom to its disappearance beyond the desert and worked away. One has to imagine how he sat up there, with a bare torso, his chest covered with hair and with very strong arms that he probably got from his ill-used father—with his wide-set eyes, his flattened nose, the parted, gray-ing beard, chewing on a piece of flatbread, also coughing occasionally from the metallic fumes of the mountain; how he hewed the tablets by the sweat of his brow, chis-eled them, planed them; how he crouched before them as they leaned against the rocky wall and, toiling pains-takingly over each detail, notched into their surfaces his chicken scratches, these runes that could do everything, after first sketching them in with his graver.

On one of the tablets he wrote:

> I, Yahweh, am your God. Thou shalt have no other gods before Me.
>
> Thou shalt make unto yourself no godlike image.
>
> Thou shalt not invoke My name in vain.
>
> Remember My day and keep it holy.
>
> Honor thy father and thy mother.

And on the other tablet he wrote:

Thou shalt not kill.

Thou shalt not commit adultery.

Thou shalt not steal.

Thou shalt not wrong thy neighbor by bearing false witness.

Thou shalt not cast a covetous eye on thy neighbor's possessions.

That was what he wrote, leaving out the resonant vowels, which were self-evident. And all the while he had the feeling that rays like a pair of horns were emanating from beneath his forelocks.

When Joshua came up the mountain for the last time, he stayed a little longer, two whole days, for Moses hadn't quite finished his work yet, and they wanted to go down together. The young man sincerely admired what his master had achieved, and comforted him about a few letters that to Moses' sorrow, in spite of the love and care he had expended, had splintered and were unrecognizable. But Joshua assured him that the overall impression did not suffer as a result.

The last thing Moses did in Joshua's presence was to coat the sunken letters with his own blood so that they would stand out better. There was no other paint at hand to do it with; he pierced his strong arm with the graver

THOMAS MANN

and carefully smeared the dripping blood into the letters so that they gleamed reddish in the stone. When the writing was dry, Moses took one tablet under each arm and gave the staff he'd been carrying to the young man. Then they climbed down together from God's mountain, toward his people's compound opposite the mountain in the wilderness.

NINETEEN

WHEN THEY had come within a certain distance of the camp and were within earshot of far-off sounds, they became aware of a muted, squealing noise, which they could not identify. Moses heard it first, but it was Joshua who mentioned it first.

"Do you hear that strange noise?" he asked. "That din? That commotion? Something's going on over there, in my opinion—a scuffle, a brawl, if I'm not mistaken. And it must be violent and widespread, since we can hear it all the way over here. If it is what I suspect it is, then it's a good thing that we're returning."

"That we're returning is a good thing in any event," replied Moses, "but from what I can make out, that's not fighting and it's not scuffling, but rather merrymaking and something like singing and dancing. Don't you hear that whooping and the banging of drums? What can have gotten into them, Joshua? Let's hurry!"

And with that, he hoisted both of his tablets higher under his armpits and strode forward more quickly, with Yehoshua shaking his head. "Singing and dancing . . . Singing and dancing . . ." he repeated over and over uneasily, and finally in open fear; for soon there could be no more doubt that it had to do not with a tussle, in which one person was lying on top and the other underneath, but rather with a united celebration, and the only question was just what had united them in such revelry.

And that was soon no longer a question, either, if it had ever been one. It was a dreadful sight. When Moses and Joshua hurried through the camp's tall timbered gate, they saw it in all its shameless clarity. The people were on the loose. They had thrown off everything that Moses had imposed upon them for their sanctification, their whole divine morality. To see them in their writhing relapse was hair-raising.

Just past the gate was an open square, free of tents, the assembly place. That's where it was happening, that's where they were carrying on, that's where they were writhing, that's where they were celebrating their miserable freedom. They all had stuffed themselves before the singing and dancing—you could see that at a glance; everywhere the square bore the traces of slaughter and gluttony. And for whom had they sacrificed, slaughtered, stuffed their bellies? There it stood. In the middle of the bare space, on a stone, on an altar pedestal it stood: an image, a piece of junk, an idolatrous absurdity: a golden calf.

It was not a calf, but a bull, the genuine, vulgar fertility-bull common to all the world's peoples. They call it a calf only because it was just moderately large, small in fact, and also poorly cast and ludicrously shaped, a clumsy atrocity, but, it must be said, all too easily recognizable as a bull. Around the piece of junk a dance of many rings was underway, a good dozen circles of men and women hand in hand, to the crash of cymbals and the beat of timbrels, their heads thrown back with eyes contorted, their knees flung to their chins, shrieking, baying, and making crassly worshipful gestures. It went in different directions, one shameless ring turning always to the right, the other to the left; in the center of the whirlwind, however, in front of the calf, you could see Aaron hopping about in the long, sleeved robe that he wore as the minister of the tabernacle and that he had gathered up to better fling about his long, hairy legs. And Miriam led the women on her timbrel.

This was merely the innermost dance around the calf; more was going on out beyond it. It is painful to acknowledge the shamelessness of the people. Some were eating slow-worms. Others lay with their sisters, and publicly, in honor of the calf. Yet others were simply sitting there and emptying their bodies, giving no thought to the little shovel. You could see men offering their strength to the bull, and somewhere one person was castigating his own mother.

THOMAS MANN

At this horrifying sight, the vein in Moses' forehead swelled to the point of bursting. With a bright red face, tearing apart the rings of the round-dance—which came staggering to a halt and whose perpetrators gawked with embarrassed grins as they recognized their master— he fought his way straight through to the calf, the core, the source, the criminal spawn. With mighty arms, he raised one of the tablets of the law high over his head and smashed it down on the laughable beast, so that its legs buckled, then hit it once again with such fury that (although the tablet broke apart, too) the piece of junk was soon a formless mass; then he swung the second tablet and put an end to the atrocity, crushing it entirely. And since the second tablet was still intact, he smashed it with one stroke against the stone pedestal. There he stood with trembling fists and moaned from deep within his breast:

"You rabble, you godforsaken people! Here lies what I brought down to you from God and what He wrote for you with His own finger, to be your talisman against the misery of ignorance! Here it lies in pieces by the wreckage of your idol. What can I tell the Lord about you now, to keep Him from consuming you?"

And he saw Aaron, the jumper, standing near him, with his eyes downcast and oily curls hanging at his neck, tall and stupid. Moses took hold of the front of his garment and shook him and spoke:

"Where did you get this golden Belial, this filth, and what did the people ever do to you so that you push them to their ruin while I was on the mountain, and prance in front of them yourself in their wretched round-dance?"

And Aaron answered:

"Oh, my dear master, do not let your wrath settle upon me or upon my sister. We had to give in. You know how bad these people are—they forced us. You delayed too long on the mountain, spent an eternity up there, so that we all thought you wouldn't return. Then the people congregated against me and cried out, 'No one knows what's become of this man Moses who led us out of Egypt. He won't be returning any more. He was probably swallowed up in the spewing maw of the mountain. Let's go, make us gods who can go before us if Amalek returns! We're a people like any other and want to let loose in front of gods who are like other peoples' gods!'—That's what they said, master, for if I may be permitted to say so, they thought they were rid of you. But tell me what I should have done, since they congregated against me? I enjoined them to bring me all the golden earrings from their ears, and I melted them down in a fire and made a mold and cast the little calf for them as their god."

"And cast it quite unrecognizably, too," interjected Moses with scorn.

"I was in such a hurry," Aaron replied, "because they wanted to have their fun on the very next day, that's today, in front of gods they could touch and feel. That's why I handed over to them what I'd cast, which does bear some resemblance, you have to admit, and they were pleased and spoke: 'Here are your gods, Israel, who led you out of Egypt.' And we built an altar in front of it, and they brought burnt sacrifices and thank-offerings and ate, and afterward they played some music and danced a little."

Moses left him standing there and made his way through the dispersed members of the round-dance back to the gate, where he stopped with Yehoshua under the rough-hewn crossbeam and cried with all his might:

"Everyone who belongs to the Lord, come to me!"

And many people came to him, those who had sound hearts and had participated reluctantly, and Joshua's armed youths gathered around the two of them.

"You miserable people," said Moses, "what have you done and how can I now atone for your sin before Yahweh so that He does not condemn you as an incorrigible, stiff-necked people and consume you? Making yourselves a golden Belial as soon as my back is turned! Ignominy upon you and upon me! Do you see the ruins over there? I don't mean the calf, it can go to hell. I mean the other ones? That is the gift that I promised you and that I brought down to you, the pithy, everlasting code, the rock of decency. It is the ten phrases that I wrote for you in God's presence in your own language. I wrote them with my blood, with the blood of my father, with your own blood did I write them. And now the gift lies in pieces."

Many of them who heard this wept, and there was a great sobbing and sniffling on the campground.

"Maybe it can be replaced," said Moses. "For the Lord is patient and greatly merciful and forgives iniquities and transgressions—and lets no one go unpunished," he suddenly thundered, as his blood shot to his head and his vein swelled again to the point of bursting. "Rather I will visit the iniquity, He said, onto the third and fourth generation as the jealous God which I am. There shall be a trial here," he cried, "and a bloody cleansing shall be decreed, for it was written with blood. The ringleaders of the group who first cried for golden gods and had the nerve to claim that the calf had led them out of Egypt, while I alone have done it, shall be extinguished—says the Lord. Whoever they are, they shall be given over to the angel of death. They shall be stoned to death and shot with arrows, even if there are three hundred of them! But let the others, meanwhile, put off all ornaments and mourn until I return—for I will go up again to God's mountain and see what I can still manage to do for you, you stiff-necked people!"

TWENTY

Moses did not attend the executions he had ordered because of the calf; the straight-backed Yehoshua took care of those. While the people mourned, he himself was on the mountain again, in front of his cave beneath the rumbling peak, and he remained another forty days and forty nights alone in the haze. But why such a long time again? It was not only because Yahweh instructed him to make the tablets again and to write the dictation into them once more—that went a little quicker this time, since he had already had some practice and, more important, had already devised the lettering. But also because, before God allowed him to proceed, Moses had to withstand a long battle with the Lord, a struggle during which choler fought with mercy, exhaustion from working fought with love for the project, and Moses had to summon up all of his persuasive powers and a clever warning call to keep God from declaring the covenant broken— thereby not only freeing Himself of the stiff-necked rabble, but demolishing it, too, just as Moses in his blazing anger had demolished the tablets of the law.

"I shall not go before them," said God, "to lead them into the land of their fathers, don't ask me to do it, I cannot guarantee my patience. I am a jealous God and flare up, and you'll see, one day I'll suddenly forget Myself and consume them in the course of our journey."

And He proposed to Moses that He would take the people, who were now as poorly cast as the golden calf and could no longer be fixed (there was no way at all to raise them up into a holy people now, there was no other recourse but to smash them to bits) . . . , He proposed that He would dash Israel to pieces and exterminate it in its present form. But He would make him, Moses, into a great people and live in a covenant with him—something Moses did not want. "No, Lord," he said, "forgive them their sins; or if not, then obliterate me from your book as well, for I do not want to survive and become a holy people in my own person instead of theirs."

And he appealed to God's honor and spoke: "Just imagine, Holy One: if You now kill these people as You would a man, then the heathen, on hearing their cry, would say: 'Bah! There was no way the Lord could bring these people into the land promised to them; He wasn't up to it. That's why He slaughtered them in the desert.' Is that what You want the peoples of the world to say about You? Therefore let the strength of the Lord grow great and by Your grace show mercy for the people's transgression!"

And it was this argument in particular that prevailed with God and persuaded Him to forgive them, but with one qualification: He declared that from Moses' generation no one but Joshua and Caleb would see the land of their fathers. "I will bring your children into it," the Lord determined, "but anyone who is more than twenty years of age shall not live to see the land. They and their bodies shall be consigned to the desert."

"All right, Lord, that will be all right," answered Moses. "Let us leave it at that." For since the decision accorded with his and Joshua's own intentions, he did not argue against it. "Now, let me renew the tablets," he said, "so that I can bring Your pithy code down to the people. In the end, it was just as well that I shattered the first tablets in anger. A few of the letters on them were spoiled anyway. I have to confess that I was secretly thinking about that when I smashed them."

And once again he sat, Joshua furtively providing food and drink, and carved and chiseled, scrubbed and planed. He sat and wrote, sometimes wiping his forehead with the back of his hand, graving and scraping the writing into the tablets—and they turned out even better than the first time. Afterward he again coated the letters with his blood, and then climbed down, the law under his arms.

And Israel was informed that it should end its mourning and put on its ornaments again—except for their earrings, of course: they had been squandered for an evil purpose. And all the people came before Moses so that he could hand over his gift to them, Yahweh's message from the mountain, the tablets displaying the ten phrases.

"Take them, my father's blood kin," he said, "and keep them holy within God's tent. But their meaning, keep it holy unto you in all that you commit and omit! For this is the compact contract and the pithy code, the rock of decency, and God wrote it into the stone with my graver, incisively, the alpha and omega of human behavior. He wrote it in your language, but in symbols that, if need be, could write all the languages of all the peoples; for He is the Lord throughout the whole world, and for that reason His is the ABC, and His language—even if it is also intended for you, Israel—necessarily becomes a language for everyone.

"Into the stone of the mountain I carved the ABC of human behavior, but it shall also be carved into your flesh and blood, Israel, so that anyone who breaks one word of the Ten Commandments shall secretly shrink back from himself and from God, and his heart shall turn cold, because he has stepped outside the limits set by God. I know well and God knows beforehand that His commandments will not be kept and that there will be transgressions against His words always and everywhere. But if any man breaks one of them, his heart shall turn ice-cold, because they are written into his flesh and blood, and he knows well that the words are binding.

"But accursed be the man who stands up and says: 'They are no longer binding.' Accursed be he who teaches you, 'Rise up and free yourselves of them! Lie, murder, and steal, whore, defile, and deliver your father and mother over to the knife, for that is human, and you should praise my name, because I proclaimed freedom to you.' Accursed be he who erects a calf and says, 'This is your god. Do all these things to honor him and circle around this piece of junk in your depraved dance!' He will be very strong, he will sit upon a golden chair and be taken for the wisest among men, because he knows that the strivings of the human heart are wicked from youth onwards. But that will be all he knows, and whoever knows only that is as stupid as the night, and it would be better if he were never born. He knows nothing of the covenant between God and mankind, which no one can breach, neither man nor God, for it is inviolable. Blood will flow in streams because of his black stupidity, so much blood that the red will fade from the cheeks of humankind, but there is nothing else to be done. The villain must be felled. And I will lift my foot, so speaks the Lord, and trample him into the mire—one hundred twelve fathoms deep into the bowels of the earth will I trample the blasphemer, and man and animal shall make an arc around the site where I trampled him, and up high in their flight the birds of the sky will swerve so that they do not fly over it. And whoever pronounces his name shall spit in all four directions and wipe his mouth and declare: 'God protect us!' Thus the earth shall be the earth once more, a vale of misery, but not a field of depravity. Everyone say Amen to that!"

And they all said Amen.

Afterword

by Michael Wood

From a distance of more than sixty-five years, the occasion of Thomas Mann's writing his novella *The Tables of the Law* (in German more simply, *Das Gesetz*, "The Law") seems to be both urgent and slightly displaced. In the midst of the war against Hitler, it was an attractive and well-intentioned idea to get ten writers to say something, each in his or her own narrative idiom, about the horrors of Nazism. Hence Armin L. Robinson's volume *The Ten Commandments: Ten Short Novels of Hitler's War Against the Moral Code* (1943). The book was designed as a response to a supposed rant of Hitler's on the subject of the commandments, late one night, some time soon after the Nazi rise to power, when he, Goebbels, Streicher, and a few others were sitting around discussing the meaning of Aryan life.

It's hard to think of this sub-Nietzschean theorizing as Hitler's worst or most dangerous fault, and by 1943 he was attacking more immediate and more tangible targets than the moral code. We might wonder, too, whether there was only one moral code for him to attack. Mann seems to have recognized this displacement straight away since his fiction, although it appeared under the title "Thou Shalt Have No Other God Before Me," concerns not a commandment but all the commandments; and more disturbingly echoes and complicates rather than simply refutes Hitler's views. Mann had read his Nietzsche too—and had read a lot more Freud than Hitler had.

The conversation, reported by Herman Rauschning, precedes the stories in the volume, and it certainly strikes several familiar, fanatical notes. "Historically speaking," Hitler says, speaking quite unhistorically, "the Christian religion is nothing but a Jewish sect. It has always been and it will always remain just that, as long as it will exist." A little later he says, "After the destruction of Judaism, the extinction of Christian slave morals must follow logically. I shall know the moment when to confront, for the sake of the German people and the world, their Asiatic slave morals with our picture of the free man, the godlike man." And then he really gets into his stride: "We are fighting against the most ancient curse that humanity has brought upon itself. We are fighting against the perversion of our soundest instincts. Ah, the God of the deserts, that crazed, stupid, vengeful Asiatic despot with his powers to make laws! That slavekeeper's whip! . . . It's got to get out of our blood, that curse from Mount Sinai."

You might think the conversation could not degenerate further than this, but it does. Both Hitler and Goebbels start rather childishly to sneer at particular commandments. Honor thy father and thy mother? Thou shalt not steal? Thou shalt not commit adultery? All so many craven restrictions on National Socialist freedom.

The commandments in Mann's novella are not the familiar, seemingly practical edicts these men are railing against, in part because the commandments in the narrative have yet to be invented by Moses or delivered to Moses by the Lord. (Mann is careful to sustain an ambiguity on this and all similar questions.) The novella tells the story of their arrival, and ends soon after this event. It is perhaps even more significant that the commandments in this work do not represent straightforward ethical concerns at all, either Asiatic or Western. They are a code of extreme, almost inhuman behavior designed to separate those who seek to follow them, whether Jews or Gentiles, from all other people on the earth. Mann's Moses is the creator of a stark, simple, almost unbearable choice: everything that isn't respect for the Ten Commandments is the loose and bestial worship of the golden calf. It is because the choice is so hard that Moses knows the commandments will often be broken:

"I know well and God knows beforehand that His commandments will not be kept and that there will be transgressions against His words always and everywhere. But if any man breaks one of them, his heart shall turn ice-cold, because they are written into his flesh and blood, and he knows well that the words are binding."

Here Mann's position, expressed through Moses, is precisely opposite that of Hitler and Goebbels, and closer to that of, say, Dostoevsky. The point is to keep the commandments when we can; and when we can't, to know what we have done. In the following paragraph, Moses seems directly to address the chattering Nazis as if they were defecting children of Israel, but even here Mann is not denying that the commandments often go against our instincts—that is in many cases what they are for:

"But accursed be the man who stands up and says: 'They are no longer binding.' Accursed be he who teaches you, 'Rise up and free yourselves of them! Lie, murder, and steal, whore, defile, and deliver your father and mother over to the knife, for that is human . . .' He knows nothing of the covenant between God and mankind, which no one can breach, neither man nor God, for it is inviolable. Blood will flow in streams because of his black stupidity . . ."

Mann's perspective, insofar as we can divine it behind his considerable irony, is not always, or even usually, so close to that of Moses. He tells us that "Moses was a very burdened man, and stayed that way ever after, burdened above all men on earth." Mann's Moses is also full of "conscientious self-reliance" (the German, *Eigenmächtigkeit*, points toward "getting one's own way").

We know from the very first lines of the novella that Moses has killed a man and enjoyed the act, found it "sweet"—later we are told "it seemed to him that he'd always had it in mind to slay somebody." It is not just a killer who devises or receives the instruction not to kill, but someone who knows the dream and the pleasure of the deed. He has a fierce, exacerbated conception of the holy. All he wants to do is to set "his father's blood kin apart for himself alone, in order to shape it and to carve unhindered a holy image of God out of the hopeless mass that he loved." Devoted to his mission, he allows his people to confuse him with his and their God, "for what he was beginning to expect of these poor souls went far beyond the human norm and could hardly have originated in the mind of a mortal." "Indeed, when he proclaimed to them that Yahweh, the Invisible One, had taken a fancy to them, he attributed to the god and located in him what might have been the god's, but was also at least in part his own . . ."

It's never clear in this work whether Moses is speaking for God or projecting a God whose authority he can borrow, and when there are hints that move in one direction rather than another they point us toward skepticism. The burning bush, for example, and the voice within it are described as the result of "inspirations and revelations, which in one particular case even broke forth from inside him and visited his soul as a flaming external vision." But the skepticism is not epistemological, or a matter of religious doubt. It represents Mann's commitment to the power of mind and passion, even pathology, with or without God's help. If God gave us the commandments, he did it through Moses. If Moses devised the commandments, he was more than human when he did it. In this perspective Moses is something of a fanatic, not a gentle humanist we can easily set up against Hitler. This is not to put Mann alongside Hitler, only to wonder, with Mann, whether humanism itself may not depend on forgotten or repressed fanaticisms.

But what about the curious phrase I quoted a little earlier, "his father's blood kin"? Is this any way to talk about Jewishness, or a Jew? The fact is, or the fact of this mischievous fiction is, that Moses is not Jewish according to the later definition of the word. He is the son of an Egyptian princess who "found" in the bulrushes the child she had ordered her maids to put there, namely, the baby she had conceived after a very swift affair with a Hebrew drawer of water. This twist in the old tale may be offensive to some, but Mann knows just what he is doing, and in certain respects seems to anticipate the polemical argument of Shlomo Sand's recent book, *The Invention of the Jewish People.* Mann's point is not that the Biblical Jewish people were invented—they had their identity from the promise made to Abraham and the prophesies of the dying Jacob—but that they were so dispersed and downtrodden in their Egyptian exile that they had to be reinvented and that Moses was the man to do the job. Indeed, he was the man who invented the idea of reinvention. He wasn't simply born into this people; he chose them because he loved them and saw their future. This is just what his God says to him:

> "Precisely because you are only half-related to them . . . you are just the man to work on them for Me and to raise them up before Me into a holy people. For if you were right there with them and were truly one of them, you would not be able to see them as they are nor put your hand to them."

The point is contentious, since Aaron and Joshua and the other leaders are Jewish by any definition, and Mann may seem to be suggesting they need a half-gentile to raise them out of their religious and cultural confusion.

What he is really saying though, I take it, and what thoroughly informs his answer to the Nazis, is that race is not destiny and that an austere moral code is not an expression of fear but of desire. The desire may be rather too symmetrically driven—as in the opening sentences of the novella: "His birth was irregular, and so he passionately loved regularity . . . His senses were hot, and so he yearned for spirituality, purity, and holiness"—and may in part represent too severe a refusal of the world of the common indication, an asceticism that is nothing but refusal. That is the danger, and this is where Nietzsche's and even Hitler's anti-Christian arguments have some purchase. But a moral code that was tilted irremediably toward refusal, as distinct from grounded in the strengths to be found in human weakness, wouldn't be moral or a code. Mann's Moses wants a God who can change the world and the people in it, who is the author of an infinitely demanding scheme in which even failure can be a form of moral progress.

Thomas Mann's many works include *Buddenbrooks*, *The Magic Mountain*, *Death in Venice*, and *Confessions of Felix Krull*. He was awarded the Nobel Prize in Literature in 1929.

Marion Faber and Stephen Lehmann co-authored a biography of the pianist Rudolf Serkin and have together translated Nietzsche's *Human, All Too Human*.

Michael Wood is the Charles Barnwell Straut Class of 1923 Professor of English and Comparative Literature at Princeton University.